The Dead Hand

Books by Michael A. Kahn

The Rachel Gold Mysteries
Grave Designs
Death Benefits
Firm Ambitions
Due Diligence
Sheer Gall
Bearing Witness
Trophy Widow
The Flinch Factor
Face Value

Other Novels
The Serena Quest

Writing as Michael Baron
The Mourning Sexton

The Dead Hand

A Rachel Gold Mystery

Michael A. Kahn

Poisoned Pen Press

Poisoned Pen Press
6962 E. First Ave., Ste. 103
Scottsdale, AZ 85251
www.poisonedpenpress.com
info@poisonedpenpress.com

Printed in the United States of America

For my nephews and nieces:
Ben, Max, Joe, Asa, Jane, Justin, Elliot, Jake, and Kate

mortmain: the influence of the past regarded as controlling the present. (From Mediaeval Latin *mortua manus*, literally "dead hand," through Old French *morte main*)

—*Merriam-Webster Dictionary*

"Man plans, and God laughs."

—*Yiddish proverb*

Section 1

"In a beautiful apple you sometimes find a worm."

—*Yiddish proverb*

St. Louis Courthouse Report

—New Lawsuits—

◇◇◇

St. Louis City Circuit Court

Caption	Description	Attorney
Danielle A. Knight v. Marsha B. Knight	Real Estate Action. Plaintiff seeks to invalidate property deed.	Thomas B. Sterling Abbott & Windsor

Chapter One

As I gazed at my newest client, I reminded myself that there is a first time for everything. I've been a lawyer now for more than a decade. Over those years I've handled plenty of oddball cases. But never one of these. I didn't even know they still existed.

"That bastard screwed me," she said, shaking her head in anger. "Good and hard."

I glanced down at the lawsuit petition on my desk and then back at my client. "You may be right, Marsha."

"May?" Her eyes widened. "I'd say definitely."

She leaned back in the chair and crossed her arms over her chest. "He totally screwed me, Rachel. You just know that when they put him into his grave he had a big grin on his face, right?"

Not being familiar with mortuary protocols, I treated her question as rhetorical.

I gestured toward the petition. "I'll need to do some legal research, Marsha. I've never had a case like this."

"I understand. My daughter told me these cases are unusual."

"Is she a lawyer?"

"Not yet. Katie's in law school. Third year. Wash U. That's how I got your name."

"Katie Knight?" The name wasn't familiar. "She knows me?"

"Oh, no. She got your name from one of her professors. She told him about my situation. She told him I needed a lawyer that was smart and tough."

"Well, well." I raised my eyebrows. "Her professor recommended me?"

"Oh, my goodness, he did more than just recommend you. He said you were tougher than every smart lawyer in town and smarter than every tough lawyer." Marsha laughed. "You ready? He told her, and I quote, 'You won't find an attorney in this town with a bigger set of *cojones* than Rachel Gold.'"

"Ah, Professor Goldberg...?"

"How did you know?"

"Wild guess."

Marsha Knight was in her fifties. Slim build, dyed-blond hair, lots of makeup, dressed in what I'd call a Full Neiman, right down to the Louis Vuitton monogram handbag and black-and-silver pumps that were either Jimmy Choo or Christian Louboutin.

Her smile faded, her lower lip quivered, and she dropped her head.

I waited.

She took a deep breath, shook her head, and exhaled. When she looked up, there were tears in her eyes.

"I don't have any savings. Zilch. If that bitch wins, I'll be left with nothing. Not even my apartment. She'd evict me. I know it."

I slid the box of Kleenex across the desk. "Here, Marsha."

She took a tissue and wiped her eyes.

Once she'd regained her composure, I guided our conversation through some easy personal topics—which for Marsha Knight included her personal trainer; her only child, Katie; and her tennis game—to the specifics of my attorney engagement agreement (including the retainer check, which she'd brought with her), and eventually back to the lawsuit.

I leafed through the petition and the attached exhibits. "So the divorce was—let's see—almost six years ago?"

"Wow, time flies."

"And this real estate deed—the document marked Exhibit A, here—it was part of your divorce settlement?"

"It was."

I skimmed through Exhibit B. "But not in the actual divorce decree."

"I think that's right. There was some technical reason. But the deed *was* recorded. I know that for a fact. I have a stamped copy from the Recorder of Deeds."

I read through the grant portion of the deed. "Who was your divorce lawyer?"

"Adam Fox."

I looked up. "Adam Fox." I frowned. "Is he the one...?"

"Yes." She sighed and shook her head. "He's the one that died."

I nodded and flipped back to the first page of the petition. "So this Danielle Knight—she's your ex-husband's widow?"

"That's her." Marsha glared as she shook her head. "Young enough to be his daughter."

We went over a few other details of the case. I explained that we'd meet again after I'd researched the legal issues. Before we parted, I asked her if there was anything else—anything at all—that I needed to know about the divorce.

She thought it over and then shook her head. "Nope."

It's the standard question every lawyer asks a new client during that initial meeting, and Marsha Knight gave me the standard answer. As I've learned over the years, the standard answer is almost always false.

Chapter Two

"*Cojones*, eh?"

"A multicultural figure of speech." Benny shrugged. "Call me bilingual, Señora."

"I'll need more than *cojones* for this one, *Señor*." I shook my head. "I didn't know these cases even existed in real life."

"Me, neither. When Katie told me about her mother's problem, I had an acid flashback to our fucking bar review course. Was it even on the goddamn bar exam?"

I thought back, trying to remember. "I don't think so. Thank goodness. I'd have blown it."

Benny Goldberg and I met many years ago as first-year associates in the Chicago office of Abbott & Windsor, then one of the largest law firms in Chicago, now one of the largest law firms in the world, with over three thousand lawyers in offices throughout the United States, Europe, and Asia. We'd been in the same bar review course that summer, along with two dozen other Abbott & Windsor newbies and hundreds of other law school grads. We all sat for the bar exam at the end of that summer.

"Do they still teach it in law school?" I asked.

"Yep. I checked with one of profs who teaches Property to the One-L's. Phoebe Hecht. She said she spends two full classes on it. The property law geeks even have an acronym for it: RAP. Win that case, woman, and you'll be known as the Rap Queen."

"Rap?"

"R-A-P."

I frowned as I silently repeated the letters and then nodded. "Ah, got it."

The Korean-American server approached our table with a full tray of food. "The Gogi Bowl?"

"Me," I said.

The server gave Benny a quizzical look. "And these burritos?"

"Yes?" Benny said.

"All three for you, sir?"

"Don't worry, pal. I'll save room for dessert."

Benny and I were having lunch at Seoul Taco, a favorite spot of ours in the University City Loop. Seoul Taco began as a food truck and expanded to a restaurant. It offers a spicy and delicious Korean take on Mexican street food. Benny's burritos, for example, had kimchi fried rice, bulgogi meat, and a special Seoul sauce. One of those giant burritos was enough for any normal person. No one has ever accused Benny of being a normal person. Among his many unique qualities, the man has capacity.

"So they still teach it, huh?" I leaned back in my chair. "What were some of those goofy law school hypotheticals?"

"Let's see." Benny squinted a moment. "There was the Case of the Fertile Octogenarian."

"That's right." I smiled. "We had that one at Harvard, too. We also had the Case of the Unborn Widow. At least that was its name. I can't remember the facts."

"My favorite was the Case of the Magical Gravel Pit."

I frowned. "Which one was that?"

"The property transfer was to be made as soon as the gravel pit ran out of gravel."

"And?"

"And when would that happen? That was the flaw. The grant might not vest for centuries."

I took a sip of iced tea and shook my head. "Ridiculous."

"Not so fast. When word about this case gets out, you'll be a goddess in that oddball legal community. A fucking trust-and-estates hottie."

"Be still my heart."

We ate in silence for a while.

Benny said, "So her ex-husband died, eh?"

"About six months ago."

"Rich, eh?"

I nodded.

"How'd he make his money?"

I smiled. "Undergarments."

"Huh?"

"Knight Apparel. Jerry was the founder and CEO. They made bras and girdles."

"Ah. The meat-packing business."

I laughed. "Not bad."

"My grandmother gets credit for that one."

"Really?"

"Back when I was growing up, my Bobba Ann worked in women's lingerie at the Bamberger's in Newark. She told people she was in the meat-packing department."

Benny took a big bite of his second burrito and chewed thoughtfully. "Knight Apparel? In St. Louis?"

"Actually, out in Sullivan. Set it up out there to avoid the unions. Hanes acquired it about fifteen years ago. Jerry Knight took the money and invested some of it in real estate."

"Such as that apartment complex."

"Exactly."

"And bought himself a trophy wife."

"So it seems."

"What about the ex-wife? Katie's mom. You like her?"

"She's okay." I took a sip of iced tea and shook my head. "She's scared. That property is her sole source of income. If she loses it, she loses everything. Including her own apartment, which is in the building."

He took another bite of the burrito and washed it down with a big gulp of soda. "You've seen the deed?"

I nodded.

"Is she fucked?"

I shrugged. "I've got to do some legal research first."

"That doesn't sound good."

I sighed. "We'll see."

Benny finished off the second burrito and unwrapped the third.

"So," I said, "you must be going on TV soon."

He gave me a surprised look. "How'd you know?"

"Your hair, boychik."

Benny and I were coaching my son Sam's kindergarten soccer team that fall. When I'd last seen Benny, at our game on Sunday afternoon, his shaggy Jew-fro had reached epic Jimi Hendrix proportions, but now it was neatly trimmed.

Benny sighed. "Fucking hair wussies at CNN."

"When?"

"A week from Wednesday. I'm on some panel for the bizarrely named Wolf Blitzer. We're going to talk about a trade regulation proposal in Congress that's giving the Silicon Valley boys irritable bowel syndrome."

"A week from Wednesday? Cool. I'll let Mom know. She's your biggest fan."

"And I'm hers. Sarah Gold is awesome."

Benny took another bite of the burrito.

Despite his national reputation in the field of antitrust law, Professor Benjamin Goldberg remains my beloved Benny. He's vulgar, he's fat, and he's gluttonous, but he's also ferociously loyal and wonderfully hilarious and my best friend in the whole world. I love him like the brother I never had. After a few years at Abbott & Windsor, we both escaped that LaSalle Street sweatshop—Benny to teach law at De Paul, me to go solo as Rachel Gold, Attorney at Law. Different reasons brought us to St. Louis. For me, it was a desire to live closer to my mother after my father died. For Benny, it was an offer he couldn't refuse from the Washington University School of Law.

Benny said, "Tell her I'll be wearing that tie she gave me for Hanukkah."

"She'll be in heaven. So will Sam. We'll be watching." I took out my iPhone and opened the calendar. "A week from next Wednesday. Got it. Oh, and you're down for dinner the following night, too. You're still coming, right?"

"You kidding? I wouldn't miss it for the world."

"Mom's making her homemade kishka for you."

"Damn, woman, I'm getting a woodie just thinking about it."

"I'll be sure to not let her know that."

He gave me a wink and took a big bite out of the burrito.

Chapter Three

RAP. The Rule Against Perpetuities.

You first hear of it in your Property class as a One L. You try to master it in your bar review course after graduation. You forget it after you sit for the bar exam. And if you're like most lawyers, you never think of it again. Ever.

I used to be one of those lawyers.

Until my meeting with Marsha Knight.

The Rule Against Perpetuities.

It was created centuries ago by the courts of England. Its purpose: to restrain the *mortmain*, which is Latin for the "dead hand." Specifically, the Rule was designed to prevent situations where the transfer of property was restricted by the hand of someone who'd been dead for decades, or even centuries. A common practice in feudal England was to put land in trust in perpetuity, with each succeeding generation living off the land without actually owning it. Why? To avoid the taxes that would be levied when the land was transferred upon the death of the owner. A perpetual trust avoided that tax. The courts created the Rule to close that loophole.

Though its roots and its original purpose were distinctly British, the Rule had crossed the Atlantic by the time of the Revolution and eventually took hold in all of the states. Turns out that the rich in the United States were just as eager as their British counterparts to control their wealth—and thus their descendants—from beyond the grave.

The Dead Hand.

The Rule Against Perpetuities can be stated in one seemingly simple sentence: "No interest in property is good unless it must vest, if at all, not later than twenty-one years after the death of some life in being at the creation of the interest." Under the Rule, the phrase "life in being" means a specified person who was alive at the time of the grant.

Sounds straightforward, albeit a little opaque.

The problem is that the Rule deals with *unknown* future events. It asks whether there is a *possibility*, no matter how remote, that the interest will not vest before expiration of that twenty-one-year period. If so, the grant fails entirely. As a result, any attempt to apply the Rule leads you down a rabbit hole of what-ifs and hypotheticals. One silly example—a favorite of law school professors—is the so-called Case of the Unborn Widow. Here's how it goes:

Our grantor leaves the property to "Jack for life, then to Jack's widow, if any, for life, and then to Jack's children." Sounds simple, eh? Brace yourself. Let's suppose Jack was married to Jill but had no children at the time of that grant. This would mean that Jack and Jill were the only Lives in Being at the time of that grant. Now let's consider one of the hypotheticals required by the Rule. If, say, Jack and Jill divorced (or Jill died) and then Jack remarried a much younger woman who was born after the date of that grant, then Jack's new wife would not be a Life in Being. As such, she could outlive Jack by more than twenty-one years. If so, the transfer to Jack's children after her death would be outside the twenty-one-year measuring period, thereby violating the Rule Against Perpetuities.

Confusing?

Agreed.

Fortunately—or, actually, unfortunately—the violation of the Rule Against Perpetuities in the case of *Danielle A. Knight v. Marsha B. Knight* was subtle but not quite as obscure as in the law school hypotheticals. It involved the grant of a succession of various interests in the Fontainebleau Estates, a luxury high-rise apartment complex in Clayton, the fashionable suburb of St. Louis. The apartment complex generated about a half-million dollars in profits a year.

Under the property deed at issue—which was dated about two months before the entry of the divorce decree in *In re the Marriage of Jerome R. Knight and Marsha B. Knight*—the Fontainebleau LLC, a limited-liability company owned by Jerry Knight, was to transfer the apartment complex to Jerry Knight not less than one week prior to entry of the divorce decree. Jerry was to hold the property as a life estate until one year after the divorce decree became a final judgment, at which point the property was to vest in Marsha Knight as a life estate but subject to forfeiture if she ever sought to modify any aspect of the divorce decree. Upon her death or forfeiture, the property was to be held jointly by the descendants of any child fathered by Jerry Knight after entry of the divorce decree.

In other words, you didn't need an advanced degree in property law to see that there were some RAP issues with that deed. For example, one hypothetical that arguably violated the twenty-one-year limit was the one that vested a life estate in Marsha Knight "one year after the divorce decree became a final judgment," since the divorce decree might *never* become a final judgment. The divorce decree *did* become a final judgment, of course, but the quirkiness of the Rule Against Perpetuities, which had been modified in other states to include a wait-and-see provision, remained in full force in Missouri.

In short, as I said to myself as I closed the Westlaw link on my office computer, Marsha Knight had a problem.

A big problem.

Chapter Four

The Cross Family Law Firm is one of the preeminent divorce firms in St. Louis, and its reception area sets its vibe and target demographic. The magazines fanned out on the coffee tables include *Vogue*, *Ms.*, and *Women's Health*. The framed movie posters feature *Erin Brockovich*, *Catwoman*, and *Kill Bill: Vol. 2*. And then there is the Norma Cross "Wall of Frames," which features photographs of Norma posing with a variety of powerful women, including Gloria Steinem, Hillary Clinton, Meryl Streep, and Olympic gold medalist Jackie Joyner-Kersee. In short, this was a divorce firm that represented women.

Norma Cross was on the shortlist of the unhappy wives of most of the rich men in St. Louis. Many of those husbands had discovered—or would soon discover—that Norma was a most painful Cross to bear. Norma Cross was also one of the more loathed members of the family practice bar—a noteworthy distinction in a field large with competition for that title. In representing her worshipful clients, Norma's arsenal included fierce aggression and brazen dishonesty. One of her longtime opponents told me that he refused to even have a telephone conference with her unless he could record it.

On the wall near the door was a framed color photograph of the late Adam Fox, Marsha Knight's lawyer in her divorce. Fox was a handsome man with sandy hair, blue eyes, a cleft chin, and a beguiling smile. The brass plaque read:

ADAM FOX
IN OUR HEARTS AND MEMORIES FOREVER

Beneath that inscription were the years of his birth and death. I did the math. He'd died at the age of 34.

"Miss Gold?"

I looked over to the receptionist. "Yes?"

"Miss Cross will see you now. Joyce will take you to her."

The receptionist gestured toward the inner doorway, where a stern, gray-haired woman in a brown checked pantsuit stood waiting.

She gave me a sour look. "Follow me."

I followed Frau Farbissina down the hallway to the large corner office.

"Ms. Cross," she announced, "I have here Rachel Gold."

Norma Cross was seated behind a glass-and-chrome desk, jotting notes on a yellow legal pad. The picture windows behind her displayed a panoramic view of the arch and the riverfront.

She removed her reading glasses, nodded at Joyce, and gave me a cold smile. "Come in."

I took the seat facing her desk.

Norma shifted her focus to her assistant, who was still in the doorway. "That'll be all, Joyce. Close the door."

I heard it close behind me.

Norma capped her fountain pen, set it on the legal pad, and leaned back in her chair. She steepled her hands under her chin and frowned. "I don't believe we've met."

"We haven't. But I've heard a lot about you, Norma."

She nodded. "And I you. You have many admirers among our colleagues."

Unable to truthfully repay that compliment, I just smiled. "That's nice."

According to the year shown on the framed St. Louis University Law School diploma on the wall, Norma Cross was in her early fifties. Whether it was good plastic surgery or good genes or a prudent combination of the two, she looked healthier and fitter and much younger than her years. She had dark brown hair cut in a wavy bob that framed a face that went well with her reputation: angular features, including prominent cheekbones, a strong nose, dark eyes, thin lips, assertive chin. She was wearing a white silk blouse with a pearl necklace and matching earrings, a navy skirt, cordovan flats, and no wedding ring.

Twice married and twice divorced, as I recalled. The first husband a state court judge, the second a hedge-fund manager. Both had—according to the news coverage of divorce cases—given Norma Cross plenty of street cred to back up the slogan featured in the full-page ads her law firm ran in the upscale suburban weeklies: "If You Deserve to Get Even, You Better Get Cross."

"So what brings you here?" she asked.

"A former client."

She raised her eyebrows, her jaw tightening. "Of mine?"

"Of your firm."

"Who?"

"Marsha Knight."

She frowned. "What about her?"

"She's been sued by her ex-husband's widow."

She shrugged. "It happens."

"The lawsuit involves a document your firm, either drafted or approved as part of the property settlement."

"And?"

"His widow is seeking to invalidate that document."

"How does that concern me?"

"The document is a real estate deed. It was the heart of the divorce settlement. It's provided my client with an annual income of nearly half a million dollars plus the apartment where she lives."

"Good for her."

"So far. But if the widow wins the lawsuit, that all vanishes. My client would be homeless and destitute."

"You still haven't told me how this is of any concern to me."

"The deed, that's how it's of concern to you. There are major flaws in that document—flaws that a diligent lawyer for Mrs. Knight should have caught and should have corrected."

"So you say. And who was that lawyer?"

"Adam Fox."

"Who's no longer here to defend himself." Her smile morphed into a sneer. "How convenient for you."

"See for yourself." I opened my briefcase, removed a copy of the deed, and slid it across the desk. "Read it."

She stared at me for a moment, eyes cold, and then picked up the document.

I leaned back in my chair and waited.

The wall to the left of the picture windows featured framed college and law school diplomas and various certificates of membership in bar and family law organizations. The other wall featured framed awards and certificates from that other side of Norma Cross—the one who competes in triathlons, places in bike races, trains in kickboxing, and climbs mountains. If that wall of plaques was meant to convey a message to her clients, then the message was clear: I will kick your husband's attorney's butt.

"Okay." She slid the copy of the deed back across the desk. "So? What's the problem?"

"The lawsuit seeks to invalidate the grant to Marsha Knight."

"On what grounds?"

"They claim it violates the Rule Against Perpetuities."

She snorted. "Are you kidding me?"

I shook my head.

"The Rule Against Perpetuities?" She shook her head. "That's a good one."

"Not if my client loses."

"Well, then, you better make sure she doesn't lose. I wish her good luck."

"I didn't come here for encouragement, Norma. If she loses, you lose." I removed an envelope from my briefcase. "I decided to deliver this in person instead of by messenger. It's a notice of a potential claim against your firm. The letter is clear: if Marsha loses her case, we're coming after your firm. You should send a copy to your malpractice carrier. Nothing personal. I'm sure the claim will be covered."

I slid the envelope across the desk. Norma ignored it, her eyes fixed on me.

I stood. "I'll be in touch."

As I reached the door, she said, "You better man up, little girl. Grow some balls and figure out how win your case. Because if you lose and you're stupid enough to come after me, I will destroy you and your spoiled cunt of a client."

I looked back as I opened the door. She was glaring at me, her face red.

"Don't be a fool, Norma. Notify your malpractice carrier."

As I started down the hall toward the reception area, she called out, "Fuck you, bitch."

I paused a moment, shook my head, and continued down the hall.

◇◇◇

"Grow some balls, eh?"

I nodded.

We were back in my office.

Jacki Brand smiled. "I'm thinking you could use co-counsel in this case. Sounds like Norma might need a good bitch slap from someone who actually cut off her own balls."

I had to smile.

Back when we first met, Jacki Brand was a big, beefy Granite City steelworker named Jack Brand who'd quit his day job to pursue his two dreams: to become a lawyer and to become a woman. I hired him/her as my legal assistant at the front end of those pursuits, back when he had just started attending law classes and taking hormone shots and needed my help in picking out appropriate dresses and shoes and a wig. The week after Jacki received her law school diploma, she underwent the surgical procedure to lop off the last dangling evidence of her original gender. When she passed the bar exam, I changed my firm's name to Rachel Gold & Associates, Attorneys at Law. Three years ago, I made her my law partner. Unaware of my plan, she had left for court that morning from the offices of Rachel Gold & Associates. When she returned, the new sign read Gold

& Brand, Attorneys at Law. You haven't experienced joy and gratitude until you've been swept off your feet in a bear hug by your blubbering six-foot three-inch, two-hundred-fifty-pound high-heeled partner.

"If Norma's smart," I said, "she'll notify her malpractice carrier once she cools down."

"She doesn't sound like the type that cools down."

I shook my head. "It's a weird situation."

"You think Marsha's case is a loser?"

I shrugged. "It'll be a challenge. That real estate deed is a mess."

"But the judge did approve it."

"Actually, he didn't. The deed was kept separate from the divorce decree. The decree had provisions for their daughter—the one in law school now—and a temporary alimony arrangement for Marsha: twenty-five thousand dollars a month for six months. But the remainder of her alimony and the property settlement were kept separate from the decree."

"Why?"

"Marsha said there was some sort of real estate tax or zoning issue that had to be cleared up. She didn't understand, but her lawyer told her it was just routine, that it would all be fine."

"And now her lawyer is dead."

"As is her ex-husband."

"What about his lawyer?"

"He's still alive."

"Who is he?"

"Irving Sliman."

Jacki's eyes widened. "You've got to be kidding. Irving Slimeball?"

"You know him?"

"I had him in a divorce case once. He's a creepy old guy. Must be at least seventy. Is he representing the widow, too?"

"No. I think he's retired. She has her own lawyer. Actually from my old law firm."

"Abbott & Windsor?"

I nodded. "A partner in their St. Louis office. Tom Sterling."

"Irving Sliman." Jacki shook her head. "Well, I'm more than happy to bitch slap Norma for you, but you got the Slimeball all to yourself.

Chapter Five

It happened just after the five-hour point. To be precise, at 3:13 p.m., according to the digital clock on the video recording. We had started the deposition at nine that morning, taken an hour break for lunch, and were a little over two hours into the afternoon portion. It occurred just after I'd shifted into my final line of questioning.

Up until then, Danielle Knight—Jerry Knight's widow, Marsha Knight's adversary—had handled herself well. Surprisingly well, considering certain assumptions I'd made before meeting her that morning. As part of my deposition preparation, I'd done some searches on Google, where I'd learned that Danielle Purcell had been a waitress at Scape restaurant in the Central West End on the night she met the recently divorced Jerry Knight, who'd been dining there with three business associates. She was twenty-three years old; he was fifty-six. They had married four months later at the Esperanza resort in Cabo San Lucas. The Google search results included a photo of the newlyweds on the beach that someone at the wedding must have posted on Facebook or Instagram or some other social media site. In that photo, the pale, balding groom wore baggy red swim trunks that showcased his ample paunch. The deeply tanned, red-haired bride wore a tiny leopard-print bikini that showcased her enormous boobs.

That photo had seemed to confirm my assumptions about Danielle Knight—most of which she shattered during the morning portion of her deposition. As I learned, she was the first member of her family to go to college, graduating with a B.A. in accounting from the University of Missouri at St. Louis. At the time she met Jerry Knight, she was working nights to pay for her second degree, a bachelor of science in nursing. Now a registered nurse, Danielle worked in the Intensive Care Unit at St. Luke's Hospital. Jerry died of a bone sarcoma two weeks before their fourth anniversary. During their marriage, she'd gotten pregnant twice, and both pregnancies had ended in miscarriages.

Up until 3:13 p.m., Danielle had maintained the calm, thoughtful, unflappable aura of an ICU nurse. She'd listened carefully to each of my questions, paused, and then provided short and direct answers. Her attorney, Tom Sterling, who usually seemed to be channeling a Clint Eastwood character from a Sergio Leone spaghetti western, had spent most of the deposition smiling and nodding as she answered each question, occasionally glancing over at me with a subtle but smug expression that, if translated into Tom's Ozark drawl, said, "Y'awl startin' to catch on here, Missy? Seem to me that client of yours is up shit's creek without no paddle."

The ten or so questions I asked leading up to the one at 3:13 p.m. concerned Danielle's knowledge of the events culminating in Jerry Knight's filing of the divorce petition, which, according to Marsha, came as a total shock. Although Tom Sterling made the obligatory "calls for speculation" and "lack of foundation" objections to each question, she was allowed to answer.

"Did he ever talk to you about his decision to file that petition?"

"Occasionally."

"And did he disclose to you that at that time he was carrying on a sexual affair with his secretary?"

Her expression visibly stiffened. "I understand that he had a relationship with another woman at the time."

"And did he tell you that he used to meet his secretary in an apartment in the same building that's at issue here, an apartment that he kept secret from his wife?"

Danielle stared at me, her face coloring.

"Objection, counselor. Irrelevant."

I returned Danielle's gaze. "You may answer, Mrs. Knight."

She leaned back in her chair and crossed her arms over her chest.

I let the silence lengthen, let her sit there scowling, knowing how that would appear on the videotape.

Finally, I said, "Do you need the court reporter to read back my last question, Mrs. Knight?"

"No."

"By 'no' do you mean you don't need the court reporter to read the question?"

"No. By 'no' I mean that Jerry never told me that."

"Do you see any problem with that behavior, Mrs. Knight?"

"What behavior?"

"Filing a petition to divorce your wife in which you accuse her of irreconcilable differences at the very same time that you're cheating on her in your secret love nest. Does that seem hypocritical to you?"

She leaned forward. "Hypocritical?" She was nearly shouting. "You want hypocritical?"

"Now Danielle," Sterling said, "no need to—"

"How about screwing your own lawyer, lady? In your own goddamn home? While your teenage daughter's bedroom is just down the hall?" She shook her head in disgust. "Your client has no shame. She deserves exactly what's going to happen to her in this lawsuit."

"How do you know that?"

"How do I know what?"

"That my client was allegedly sleeping with her divorce lawyer?"

"Sleeping?" She snorted. "You mean fucking like two rabbits in heat?"

"Danielle…" Sterling warned.

"I repeat my question? How do you know that?"

"Objection," Sterling said. "Counselor, I'm gonna have to instruct my client not to answer."

"Oh?" I said to him. "On what grounds?"

Sterling paused, frowning. "Um, spousal privilege."

I shook my head. "Really, Tom?"

"How do you think I know?" Danielle shouted.

"Danielle," Sterling warned.

"Jerry told me! That's how I know."

"Time out," Sterling stood. "We're taking ourselves a little break here. I'm going to need to have a word or two with my client out there in the hall."

Chapter Six

I clicked the PAUSE button and turned to Marsha Knight.

She was staring open-mouthed at the screen, at the frozen image of Danielle's enraged face. The time clock on the lower right corner of the screen read 3:17 p.m.

Marsha and I were seated on opposite sides of the table in my conference room, the video screen mounted on the wall.

"Is that true?" I said.

Marsha looked over at me, back at the screen, back at me, and then lowered her head.

"Well?"

She nodded, head down.

"You heard her testimony, Marsha. She said your ex-husband told her. How did he know?

She shook her head.

"Look at me, Marsha."

She raised her head, tears in her eyes.

"Did Jerry ever mention it to you?" I asked.

She shook her head.

"What about his lawyer? Irving Sliman. Did he ever say anything to you?"

She shook her head.

"And your own lawyer? Adam Fox? Did Adam ever mention it?"

She shook her head.

I leaned back in my chair. "When did it start?"

She took a deep breath and sighed. "I'm not sure."

"Before or after you retained him as your attorney?"

"Oh, after. Definitely after. Maybe a month or two after."

"Had you known him before that?"

"No. I had a friend who got divorced. She'd hired the Cross Family Law Firm. Adam had represented her. She recommended them both to me—Norma and Adam."

"How long did your affair last?"

"Maybe six months, maybe a little longer."

"Did it last beyond the divorce decree?"

"No. We ended it before that."

"Who ended it?"

She shrugged. "I guess we both sort of did."

"Why?"

She frowned. "I'm not sure. It just seemed like it wasn't such a great idea, him being my lawyer and all."

"Is that what he said?"

"Maybe. We talked about it, though. I guess we both agreed." She shrugged. "Maybe him more than me."

"And he never said anything about your husband—about Jerry knowing about your relationship?"

"No. Never."

"And your husband never said anything to you?"

"No. No one did. I had no idea anyone else knew." She sighed again, her lips quivering. "I just felt so alone, Rachel. Just old and pathetic and alone. You have no idea. And there he was. Adam was so good to me, so protective."

She gave me a sad smile. "And so handsome. That first time… it was like magic. So much different than making love to Jerry, so much better. God, better than anything I'd ever experienced. I felt young again. Sexy, again. Jesus, listen to me. How pathetic. I'm a goddamn cliché."

"Did your daughter know?"

She looked back at the screen for a moment and then turned to me. "I don't know. Maybe. We never talked about it. Ever." She shrugged. "But maybe."

"Did he ever spend the night at your house?"

"Usually not. But sometimes he'd fall asleep after we made love and I wouldn't wake him. I should have, of course. It was stupid of me. Selfish, too. But it was so nice to have him in the bed with me, to snuggle with him."

"You said you broke up before the divorce was final."

She nodded.

"What about after?"

"What do you mean?"

"Did you ever have contact with him after the divorce?"

"No." She sighed again. "I was hoping he'd call me. He never did. And four or five months later he was dead."

"Did you go to his funeral?"

She nodded. "It was so sad, Rachel. His parents were there. His sister was there. All of his friends. He was so young. It was such a tragedy."

After a moment, I turned toward the video screen and clicked the OFF button. The screen went blank.

"What does this mean for my lawsuit?" Marsha asked.

"I'm not sure."

An hour later I was going over my research notes on the relevant Missouri case law on the Rule Against Perpetuities when Dorian, my assistant, cleared her throat.

"Rachel?"

I looked up. Dorian stood in the doorway. "Yes?"

"Ms. Mulligan is here."

"Please show her in, Dorian."

I sighed.

Zombies.

Two in one month.

But this time I had the trophy widow.

Section 2

"As long as a man lives, the entire world is too small for him; after death, the grave is big enough."

—*Yiddish proverb*

St. Louis Courthouse Report

—New Lawsuits—

◇◇◇

St. Louis County Circuit Court

Caption	Description	Attorney
In re Estate of Bertram R. Mulligan	Petitioner Bertram R. Grimsley (nee Mulligan) seeks order invalidating bequest to decedent's widow's child	Milton Strauss Smilow & Wortz

Chapter Seven

Their lawyers call them "high-net-worth individuals prepared to shoulder the responsibility for providing wealth for future generations and essential funding for important causes even after they are no longer with us."

Benny calls them zombies.

And since zombies are already dead, they're hard to kill. Especially Bert Mulligan. According to his obituary, the letters DFWB were tattooed on his right arm, and they were still there when they lowered his casket into the grave. The G-rated translation: Don't Fool With Bert.

But I'm getting ahead of my case notes.

The first entry is dated October 19, the afternoon of the same day I showed Marsha Knight the videotape of Danielle Knight's deposition.

Although Cyndi Mulligan and I already knew one another, this was our first attorney-client meeting. We'd met a month earlier in our pediatrician's waiting room. Sam and I were there for his five-year checkup. Cyndi and her daughter, Carson, were there for Carson's one-year checkup. Only our doctor was missing. She was on an emergency call at the nearby hospital, which meant that Cyndi and I had the opportunity to become acquainted, especially since our only alternative was to learn the latest on the Kardashian sisters, whose images were on the covers of all four issues of *People* and *US* on the magazine rack.

That was then. One month later, Cyndi was seated in the chair facing my desk, her eyes red, a tissue clutched in her hand, her voice quavering.

"Please help me, Rachel."

Cyndi and I shared something else in common: we were both widows. Cyndi was the famous one, at least by St. Louis standards. Her husband had been Bert Mulligan, the founder and ruthless CEO of The Mulligan Group, a conglomerate headquartered in St. Louis that owned companies in various industries around the world. At the time of his death, Mulligan was number two hundred forty-seven on the *Forbes Magazine* list of the four hundred wealthiest Americans.

Bert had referred to Cyndi as his personal "mulligan," which the dictionary defines as a free shot given to a golfer when his previous one was poorly played. Bert's first marriage had lasted three decades and produced one angry son and one bitter ex-wife. Several years after that divorce, Bert spotted the blond and blue-eyed Cyndi on the sidelines at a St. Louis Rams football game, where she was a Rams cheerleader. It was, at least according to their wedding invitation (still displayed on Cyndi's Facebook page), "love at first sight." Bert was seventy-two, and Cyndi was twenty-six.

Nevertheless, they wowed their wedding party guests with their first dance as husband and wife. Disdaining the usual romantic slow dance, Bert took his bride onto the dance floor to his favorite Rolling Stones song, "Start Me Up." The large crowd clapped and cheered as the newlyweds did an acrobatic swing dance through the song's closing line, when Mick Jagger tells the object of his affection that "you'd make a dead man come."

It was, as I would learn, an eerie bit of prophecy.

Cyndi shook her head in disgust. "He is such a hateful man."

"Bert Junior?" I asked.

She nodded. "Did you know he changed his name?"

"To what?"

"Grimsley. His mother's maiden name. He's now Bert Grimsley."

"When did this happen?"

"Before I met his father. Right after they had that falling out at work."

Falling out at work.

I had to smile. Like calling World War II a squabble.

Nine years ago, the festering hostilities in the Mulligan family erupted onto the front page when Bert Junior tried to pull off a hostile takeover of his father's company. The scheme collapsed in spectacular fashion when Junior's supposed co-conspirators sold him out just before the key meeting of the board of directors. He strode into that meeting as General Counsel and Vice-President, confident he would emerge as CEO and Chairman of the Board. An hour later, he staggered out unemployed and holding court papers naming him as the defendant in the company's multi-million-dollar breach-of-fiduciary-duty lawsuit. He literally had to beg the receptionist to call him a cab, since the company had already deactivated his cell phone and seized his Mercedes-Benz company car. He and his father never spoke again.

DFWB.

Cyndi dabbed at her eyes with the handkerchief. Though she was pretty in that classic Midwest cheerleader version of pretty, there was an almost childlike sweetness that you sensed the moment you met her. As with the other Rams cheerleaders, that role had been a weekend gig for her. Before marrying Bert, Cyndi had been a nursery school teacher.

"So he's now Bert Grimsley," I said. "What's his issue with you?"

She twisted the handkerchief in her hands. "He claims Carson isn't Bert's daughter."

I chose my words carefully. "Why would that matter to him?"

"Because of Bert's will."

Oy, I said to myself as I settled back in my chair.

The dead hand.

Chapter Eight

"...and into the night of his very own room," I read, "where he found his supper waiting for him." I turned the page. "And it was still hot."

I closed the book, leaned over, and gave Sam a gentle kiss on his forehead. "Goodnight, Smoochy."

I turned toward Yadi, who was in his usual bedtime position curled up on the comforter at the foot of Sam's bed. Yadi was our collie-shepherd mix—one straight German shepherd ear, one floppy collie ear, and a gentle temperament unless you were a stranger approaching Sam or me, at which point he morphed into a junkyard attack guard.

I scratched Yadi on the head. "Goodnight, buddy."

He flopped his tail three times and settled his head back down on the comforter.

As I stood, Sam said, "Mommy, could Uncle Benny come say goodnight?"

I smiled. "I'm sure he can. I'll go tell him."

I came down the stairs to find Benny and my mother at the kitchen sink—my mother doing the washing, Benny the drying. They were talking about Benny's appearance on CNN the night before—an appearance that I'd watched with my mother and Sam. Benny had been, as usual, brilliant and funny and unflappable.

"That girl on the panel..." my mother was saying. "The cute one named Lauren from the chamber of commerce. Is she single?"

"Give me a break, Sarah. Did you hear what she was saying? She's makes Ayn Rand sound like a socialist."

"Don't be so dismissive, Mr. Big Shot Professor. That girl is cute and she's smart, and—with a last name of Becker—I'm pretty sure she's Jewish. Talk to that man on the show. He must have her phone number."

"What man?"

"The host. That Blintz guy."

Benny chuckled as he glanced over at me. "It's Blitzer, Sarah, not blintz. He's a talking head, not a pancake."

"Blitzer? He might be Jewish, too."

"Great. Wolf Blitzer as my yenta."

"Don't laugh. Talk to him. She's a nice Jewish girl."

"Excuse me," I said.

They both turned.

"Uncle Benny, Sam wants to know if you could say good-night."

He grinned. "Absolutely."

"Give me the dish towel," I said. "I'll dry."

◇◇◇

We were having tea and my mom's kamishbroit for dessert. Kamishbroit is a deliciously crunchy Yiddish cousin of the Italian *biscotti*. Benny had already consumed almost half the platter.

I'd filled them in on Marsha Knight's case—including Marsha's affair with her divorce attorney and my prior delightful meeting with Norma Cross, including Norma's charming send-off, which made my mother so angry that she was ready to drive to her office and slap her in the face—not a prudent idea, I had explained, when the target of your slap has won two tournaments in kickboxing. Moreover, I told her, she'd have to get in line behind Jacki Brand.

As for my other "dead hand" case—the one for Cyndi Mulligan—I'd brought the file home with me to work on later that night. After Benny had returned from Sam's bedroom, he asked to see the Last Will and Testament of Bert Mulligan.

He finished reading it, tossed the document onto the table, took a sip of tea, and shook his head in disgust. "Zombies."

He reached for another kamishbroit and raised it in respect toward my mother, who nodded and smiled. He consumed it in two big bites and turned to me. "What the fuck is a bloodline trust?"

"We'd have known the term if we'd taken trusts-and-estates in law school."

"Thank God for that." He took a sip of tea and reached for another kamishbroit. "So enlighten your mother and me, Gorgeous."

"A bloodline trust is a way to pass on wealth to your kids while protecting it from others outside the family."

My mother frowned. "What does that mean?"

"Let's say Sugar Daddy establishes a million-dollar bloodline trust for Sonny Boy. Sonny Boy gets married, and five years later he gets divorced. No kids in the marriage. The ex-wife is entitled to half the marital assets, but those assets don't include whatever is in the bloodline trust, which stays with Sonny Boy."

"Thus the pretentious phrasing." Benny flipped back through the trust. "Here we are. Page four. 'If my wife Cyndi Raimey Mulligan shall give birth to a child in my bloodline…'" He looked up with a grin. "A child in my bloodline? A tad high-faluting for the son of a lead miner."

I shrugged. "I'm just a simple trial lawyer."

"With a tush and legs to die for." He turned to my mother. "Agreed?"

She nodded. "She's a real beauty, my Rachel."

Benny turned to me. "So what happens if your client gives birth to a child not in his bloodline?"

I shook my head. "That's the odd part."

"How so?"

"There's no provision for that."

"What do you mean?"

"Bert Mulligan's estate plan—the will, the trusts, the other stuff—totals more than two hundred pages, but there's nothing in all of those documents about what happens if Cyndi has a child outside his bloodline."

"Nothing?"

"Nothing."

Benny frowned. "Sounds like the lawyer screwed up."

"He didn't," I said. "I talked to him today. He told me Bert made him take that provision out of the papers."

"No way."

"Way. He showed me the draft. There are almost two pages of provisions dealing with what happens if a child is born outside the bloodline. They're all X'ed out. The lawyer was so nervous, he made Bert put his initials next to each deleted provision"

"Did Bert say why he wanted those provisions removed?"

"Not according to his lawyer."

"When did he do his estate plan?"

"His lawyer said he drafted the original documents shortly after the wedding. Bert came back about a year before he died to have him create the bloodline trust."

"Did he give a reason?"

"Sort of. The lawyer said that Bert mentioned that he'd recently seen his cardiologist, who was worried that he was at high risk for another heart attack. He'd had two prior ones."

"That's how he died, right? While schtupping his cheerleader wife?"

"My goodness," my mother said. "Is that true?"

I smiled. "He did die of a heart attack, Mom. I looked up the obituary in the *Post-Dispatch* this afternoon. It said, quote— 'according to his widow, Mr. Mulligan died in her arms in bed'—close quote." I turned back to Benny. "I haven't asked Cyndi about the details."

"Wonder if that was the night she got pregnant?" Benny grinned. "That's what I'd call going out with a bang." He took a sip of tea. "So what happens if her kid doesn't qualify under that trust?"

"Cyndi's part stays the same. She has her own trust that takes good care of her for the rest of her life. But the bloodline trust is where all the assets go, including the stock in The Mulligan Group. According to the lawyer, if Bert Junior can break that trust, then Junior and his mother inherit everything, including the stock in The Mulligan Group."

Benny raised his eyebrows. "Damn, girl, you may have a real shit storm on the horizon. What's next?"

"I'll find out tomorrow morning."

"Oh? What's tomorrow morning?"

"That's when I meet with Junior."

Benny left after dessert, and my mother and I cleaned up. Fortunately, my mother lives about twenty steps from my back door. More precisely, she lives in the renovated coach house behind my house. After my husband, Jonathan, died, my mother sold her condo and, God bless her, moved in to help me raise Sam and my two stepdaughters, Leah and Sarah. Leah is now in her senior year at Brandeis University, and Sarah is a freshman at Johns Hopkins University.

"I talked to Sarah this afternoon, Mom."

"How's my doll baby doing?"

"She sounds good. She's made friends, she likes her classes, she likes her roommate, she even likes Baltimore."

"Oh, thank goodness."

Three weeks ago, I'd gone up to Baltimore with my step-daughter to move her into her freshman dorm at Hopkins. During the move-in, I'd met her roommate, Chelsea, who seemed nice, and I'd watched with pleasure as Sarah ran into three freshmen girls on campus who she'd already connected with on Facebook. The two of us had a delicious seafood dinner in the Fell's Point area that night and a tearful goodbye the next morning. We'd talked or texted every day since then.

"Parents Weekend is next month," I said. "The weekend of the fifteenth."

"I hope you're going."

"Definitely."

"Good. You should."

I shut off the faucet and turned to my mother. "She wants you to come, too."

"Me?"

I nodded. "She said to me, 'Could Baba come?' I told her I'd ask."

My mother's eyes watered. "She wants me there. She said that?"

I smiled. "Yes, she did. And you're coming."

I gave her a hug.

Although my two stepdaughters call me Rachel, they call my mother Baba, which is Yiddish for grandmother. Their Baba is hardheaded and opinionated and sets high standards for her grandchildren. Don't ask the two girls how many times their redheaded Baba made them rewrite their college application essays. Though she can exasperate me like no other human on the face of the Earth, we all adore her.

My mother came to America from Lithuania at the age of three, having escaped with her mother and baby sister after the Nazis killed her father, the rest of his family, and whatever semblance of religious faith my mother might ever have had. Fate remained cruel. My mother—a woman who reveres books and learning—was forced to drop out of high school and go to work as a waitress when her mother (after whom I'm named) was diagnosed with terminal liver cancer. My Grandmother Rachel died six months later, leaving her two daughters, Sarah and Becky, orphans at the ages of seventeen and fifteen. Two years later, my mother married Seymour Gold, a gentle, shy, devoutly Jewish bookkeeper ten years her senior. My sweet father was totally smitten by his beautiful, spirited wife and remained so until his death from a heart attack almost ten years ago on the morning after Thanksgiving.

Still hugging her, I said, "So put it on your calendar, Mom."

She nodded, squeezing me even harder.

Chapter Nine

"The one thing I did learn from my father, Miss Gold, is that when you have the upper hand, you don't ease up until you've crushed your opponent."

Bert Grimsley (née Mulligan) gave me a smile that looked more like a sneer. "Welcome to my father's rules."

We were seated in a conference room at Smilow & Wortz, a bottom-feeder collections law firm where Bert Grimsley had landed after (1) the $8 million verdict against him in The Mulligan Group lawsuit, and (2) the related hearing before the Missouri Attorney Disciplinary Commission, which suspended his law license.

Grimsley was seated directly across from me. To his left (my right) sat his mother, Dorothy, to his right was a lawyer named Milton Strauss. Strauss was in his sixties, a hefty man in a wrinkled gray suit and a bright orange tie with a brown gravy stain. He sported a thick white goatee and a smile like a satyr's leer. In contrast, Grimsley's mother was thin, dour, and stiff in her designer outfit and heavy gold jewelry. She sat with her head tilted back on a long neck, peering down her nose, eyes blinking, like some exotic bird. She may have once been beautiful, but too many years in the sun had left deep wrinkles in her face and splotches on her leathery neck.

Bert Grimsley said, "Word is that your client actually fucked him to death." He glanced to his left. "Pardon my French, Mother."

His mother fluttered her eyelids, pursed her lips, and leaned back even further.

Bert Grimsley turned to me. "If that's true, then the bastard got a better exit than he deserved."

I didn't reply.

Bert Grimsley squinted at Strauss. "Milton will give you a courtesy copy of the petition. We filed it under seal in the hope, perhaps naïvely, that the gold digger might prefer to settle this ugly matter quietly."

Strauss slid a court-stamped copy of the petition across the table. "Here you go, kiddo."

I kept my eyes on Grimsley. "What ugly matter?"

Grimsley gave me a tight smile. "The child, of course. And the consequences flowing therefrom, as we lawyers like to say."

"*We* lawyers? Has your law license been restored?"

His smile vanished. "Yes, Miss Gold. *We* lawyers."

Bert Grimsley resembled photos I'd seen of his father. With their bald heads, bulbous noses, and tendency to squint, they seemed haughty versions of the cartoon character Mr. Magoo. Unlike Mr. Magoo, however, father and son were tall and athletic. Indeed, both had played college basketball—Bert Sr. at Southeast Missouri State, Bert Jr. at Tufts.

I glanced at the cover page of the petition. "So you claim the child isn't his?"

"Precisely."

"Leaving to one side the merits of that claim, what if you are correct?"

"The trust is void, and—*voila!*—I inherit everything. Mother and I do, to be precise."

He turned to his mother with a smile. She peered over at him, unsmiling, and blinked.

I said, "You mentioned a settlement proposal. What is it?"

"We'll let the bitch keep the trust he set up for her."

"How does Mrs. Mulligan's trust have anything to do with this dispute?"

He gestured toward the petition. "My father had the gall to accuse me of breach of fiduciary duty." He forced what sounded like a snicker. "Turnabout's fair play. Isn't that right, Milton?"

Milton gave me a smirk. "It's all laid out right there in that court filing, young lady. Every last dirty detail."

I put the petition into my briefcase, snapped it shut, and stood.

"One final question." I said. "You claim that Mr. Mulligan is not the biological father of the girl, correct?"

"Bingo."

"What is the basis for your contention?"

Bert grinned. "Simple math."

"Meaning?"

"Meaning my father died on April first. The child was born the following February fourteenth. Last time I checked, Miss Gold, the gestation period for a human is nine months. The child was born almost eleven months after April first."

He leaned forward, his grin now a smirk.

"To put it in plain English, girl, I ain't no April fool."

I stared down at him as I picked up my purse. "I bet you've been practicing that silly line all morning. It still sounds lame."

I turned and left.

Chapter Ten

Cyndi shuddered. "He is such a nasty man."

I had just filled her in on my meeting with Bert Junior, his mother, and their attorney, Milton Strauss.

"It gets even nastier," I said. "He's also trying to invalidate the trust that your husband set up for you. There's no merit to that claim, Cyndi, I promise. It's just a pretext to include a lot of nasty allegations about you."

"What kind of allegations?"

"Undue influence. False pretenses. Sexual enticement. That sort of thing."

I could see the anger flare in her eyes.

"Rachel, I don't care about that stuff. That creep can say whatever he wants about me. I'll be just fine. This is about my daughter." She leaned forward. "*Our* daughter."

"I agree." I uncapped my fountain pen and pulled over a legal pad. "Let's talk about your daughter. Let's talk about those eleven months."

She nodded. "She's Bert's child. I had sex with no one else back then, and I haven't had sex with anyone since Bert died. I loved that man, Rachel. I loved him. And I adore our daughter. She's my dear husband's legacy."

"So tell me about the lag time."

She took a deep breath and let it out slowly. "Okay."

◇◇◇

"Really?" Benny laughed. "Sounds like Mr. Grim Reaper is in for a surprise."

"I hope so."

Benny had dropped by my house around seven-fifteen, as he did most Wednesday nights after teaching his advanced antitrust seminar. I'd already fed Sam, given him a bath, and gotten him ready for bed. Sam looked forward to these Wednesday nights even more than I did because that's when his Uncle Benny arrived just in time to read him a book and put him to bed. As usual, Benny showed up with a ridiculous amount of takeout—this time from one of our favorite Thai restaurants—plus a six-pack of Urban Chestnut's Winged Nut Ale.

After Benny put Sam to bed, I filled him in on the latest developments as he virtually inhaled an order of fish cakes.

"Assuming that douchebag doesn't drop his suit," he said, "how will you prove that Bert Senior is the kid's father?"

"I'm going to serve a subpoena on the sperm bank. I'll ask for a copy of all their records. Seems the quickest way to end this."

Benny scarfed down a forkful of pad thai. "So when did old Bert tell her about the frozen treat?"

"About a year before he died. They'd been trying to get pregnant since the wedding. Nothing. She really wanted a baby, and so did he. He went to his urologist. They did some tests. Results showed he had a low sperm count. Not hopelessly low, but low enough to seriously reduce his odds of ever getting her pregnant."

Benny cracked open another bottle of beer. "So when did the old guy make those, uh, deposits?"

"He told her he did it ten years earlier."

"Why?"

"He didn't go into detail with her, and she doesn't actually know. He would have been in his early sixties. She thinks maybe he was worried that if he ever remarried he might be too old to father a child."

"Makes sense," Benny said. "Powerful rich guys are obsessed

with sowing their seed. Think of how many of those *alter kockers* become fathers again in their seventies."

"I did a little research online. Assuming Cyndi has the dates right, Mulligan would have made his sperm deposits about a year after The Mulligan Group acquired Unisource Laboratories."

"Okay. So?"

"One of Unisource's divisions is Procreative Cryogenics. Sperm banks are a big part of their operations. Who knows? Maybe that acquisition gave him the idea to store some of his own, just in case. Whatever the reason, he told Cyndi about the sperm bank. He told her how she could obtain his specimens. He made her promise that if he died and she wasn't pregnant, that she would get herself artificially inseminated. He told her there should be enough for at least two tries. She got pregnant the second time."

I opened the container of red curry with shrimp. "Great choice. I love their curry."

"That's why I got it, woman." He took a gulp of beer. "So Bert Junior was right about the timing, though. She definitely got pregnant *after* he died. Does that still qualify under that crazy trust?"

"Absolutely. The trust doesn't specify any time period. Remember the language: 'If my wife, Cyndi, shall give birth to a child in my bloodline...' That's all that's required."

Benny laughed. "She could have really messed with Junior's head. Hell, she could have waited a few years before getting a shot of the old fart's jizz."

"You're such a romantic. Actually, Cyndi said that Bert made her promise to do it right away. I'm sure he didn't want her stuck in the middle of some freak show."

"Which she is anyway."

I sighed. "What a mess."

That, I would soon discover, was an understatement.

Section 3

"Empty barrels make the most noise."

—*Yiddish proverb*

Chapter Eleven

One explanation for the judge's temperament was his most unfortunate combination of height (barely five feet) and name. It did seem a plausible explanation. After all, little Harry Ballsack must have suffered plenty of teasing on the middle school playground and in the high school locker room. But now, three decades later, perched high above the lawyers on his judicial bench, clad in a black robe, and clasping a gavel in his little hand, every day was payback time for the Honorable Judge Ballsack.

He sneered down at the young lawyer.

"Are you serious, Counsel?" he demanded in his high-pitched, nasal voice.

The young lawyer looked down at his notes, frowned, and then looked back up at Judge Ballsack. "Yes, Your Honor. We are serious."

"Did you take torts in law school?"

"Yes, Your Honor."

"And you passed?"

"Yes, Your Honor."

"Well, you might want to call that professor and ask for a tuition refund because you certainly flunked today." He banged the gavel. "Motion denied! Next."

Down below, his courtroom clerk, a plump black woman named Josephine, ran her finger down the docket calendar and called out, "Knight versus Knight. Defendant's motion to compel."

The three of us—me in the middle, Tom Sterling to my left, Norma Cross to my right—approached the podium. Judge Ballsack scowled at Tom, who was the judge's physical opposite. The judge was short and Tom was tall. The judge was pudgy with a double chin and Tom was lanky with a lantern jaw. The judge was bald, had beady little eyes, a big nose, and a pencil-thin black mustache. Tom had thick silver hair, a matching goatee, and the facial structure of a cowpoke from an old Western movie. He was even wearing a bolo tie—a rare fashion accessory in the Circuit Court of St. Louis County.

Still scowling at Tom, the judge said, "What do you want, Sterling?"

Tom chuckled and raised his hands, palms facing the judge. "Your Honor, I'm just spectating today. Don't have a dog in this fight."

I cleared my throat. "Rachel Gold, Your Honor, for the defendant. This is my motion."

The judge frowned at me and then glanced to my right. "Ms. Cross? Why are you here?"

Norma gave him a friendly smile. "Against my will, Your Honor."

She took a step to the side of the podium, having dressed for the occasion and, apparently, for this judge, whose glare faded as his eyes moved down from her face. Her sweater top was cut low, her skirt was hemmed short, and her heels were high.

"Ms. Cross is here," I said, pausing until Ballsack shifted his gaze back to me, "because we have served her firm with a subpoena to produce my client's file. Ms. Cross has failed to produce that file, and she has failed to respond to several written requests I sent her, each of which is attached to my motion as an exhibit. There are four such requests. Accordingly, we seek an order from the Court compelling her to produce that file."

The judge frowned. "Why exactly do you think that Ms. Cross would have your client's file?"

"Because her law firm represented my client in the divorce case. Because her law firm negotiated and approved the deed of trust that is at issue in *this* case. And because that file belongs to my client. As discovery has shown here, that file will likely contain highly relevant evidence—evidence this Court will need in rendering its decision."

The judge turned to Norma Cross and tugged on the flesh below his double chin. "Well? She seems to have a point there."

Norma sighed and shook her head. "Miss Gold really needs to show some restraint. The answer is simple. We can't produce what we don't have."

Judge Ballsack frowned. "Come on now, Miss Cross. Are you seriously trying to tell this Court that you don't have your own client's file?"

"Former client, Your Honor. Former. We certainly did have that file when we represented her. Absolutely. But that divorce was final almost six years ago. I brought with me today a copy of our standard form engagement letter."

She handed one to his courtroom clerk and then gave Tom and me a copy.

"As the Court will see," she continued, "that letter clearly states to our clients that we will maintain their files in our storage facility at our expense for five years after their case is closed, but that after those five years—unless they have requested their file within that period—the materials will be discarded. Of course, if they request their file during the period, we will have it delivered to them. Alas, Mrs. Knight failed to request her file, and thus it was destroyed in the ordinary course of business, along with any electronic documents related to that file. I can assure Miss Gold that there is no danger of any privileged communications from that file falling into Mr. Sterling's hands, since we are diligent in insuring that all such abandoned files are shredded."

She turned to me and shook her head in feigned reproach. "You should apologize, young lady, for wasting this Court's valuable time. And mine. Enough is enough." She turned back to the judge with a smile. "That's all, Your Honor."

Before I could respond, the judge slammed down his gavel. "Motion denied! Next."

Chapter Twelve

I placed the white stone on top of Jonathan's headstone, right next to the one that Sam and I had placed two Sundays ago. I took a deep breath, laid my hand on the cool granite, and closed my eyes.

After a moment, I shook my head and exhaled, "She's horrible, Jonathan. Even worse than I thought."

I'd planned on coming to the cemetery after the court hearing that morning, but not because of the hearing. I had good news to share with my late husband—good news about his two daughters—and the St. Louis County Courthouse was just ten minutes away from the cemetery.

But Norma Cross had darkened my thoughts on the drive over. I assumed she had lied to the judge, and I also assumed that I'd never be able to prove it. She'd destroyed Marsha Knight's divorce file, and I was sure that she'd done that *after* I'd had her served with the subpoena for that file. The judge hadn't bothered to look at the document she'd claimed was her law firm's form engagement letter—the one that supposedly allowed the firm to destroy a client's files after five years—but I'd studied my copy. There was nothing about that document—which was literally a fill-in-the-blanks form—that indicated when it was created, *i.e.*, it could have been created the day before the hearing.

But the more important question—the more perplexing question—was *why* Norma Cross had destroyed Marsha's divorce file. Was she just being obstinate, or had there been something in that file that she deemed harmful to her or her firm?

I'd called my client from outside the courthouse right after the hearing. Marsha Knight checked her file and called me back as I was pulling into the cemetery. She didn't have a copy of any such engagement letter in her file. But, I reminded myself, Marsha's records from the divorce were so spotty that the absence of an engagement letter wasn't evidence one way or the other.

But enough about Norma Cross, I told myself as I turned from the gravestone.

At the foot of the two graves was a granite memorial bench with WOLF carved on the front. I took a seat there and tried to get my thoughts and my emotions under control.

Spending time at Jonathan's grave gave me comfort, even though there was plenty there for discomfort, beginning with the side-by-side headstones of my husband and his first wife. The pair of dates etched onto each headstone was stark evidence of life's unfairness. Robyn Wolf died of ovarian cancer at the age of thirty-three, leaving behind two young daughters. Jonathan Wolf died ten years later at the age of forty-four. He'd been determined to get home from a two-week trial in Tulsa in time for our wedding anniversary. Rather than wait for the next commercial flight, which included a change of planes in Kansas City and a one-hour layover that wouldn't get him home until eleven that night, he'd hitched a ride on his client's corporate jet, which took off in a thunderstorm and crashed ten miles east in an oilfield, killing all aboard.

Jonathan had been an Orthodox Jew. I'm raising his daughters and our son in the Jewish tradition, albeit at my Reform congregation. I still light the candles and say the blessings on Friday night and go to shul to say Kaddish on his yahrzeit and on my father's yahrzeit, but Jonathan's death—coupled with his first wife's death and the tragedies that have befallen some of my friends—have made me wonder whether the only religion that makes sense out of life's nonsense is the religion of the ancient Greeks. In a world ruled by a rowdy mob of egotistical deities, bad things happen to good people and good things happen to bad people because that's how they roll up on Mount Olympus.

The other disquieting aspect of the paired gravesites is their location. To the left of Robyn's headstone is a double headstone for her father (who had died two years before Robyn) and her mother (who was still alive), and to the left of those headstones is an entire row of tightly packed gravesites. To the right of Jonathan's headstone stands a large memorial for the Schwartz family, several of whom are buried in a row. The result, when I sit alone on the memorial bench, is an acute sense of solitude. There is no room for me.

But with any luck, I told myself, that won't be an issue for many decades.

"Guess who's going to be a doctor?" I said softly. "Leah's taking the MCATs this Saturday. Your mom would have been so proud."

Leah was the older daughter, now in her senior year at Brandeis University. She'd been wavering for months between medical school and a graduate program in biochemistry—a decision that she and I had spent hours on the phone discussing. She called last Sunday to announce that she'd opted for medicine.

"And Sarah loves Hopkins. She's having a wonderful time. We're all going up for Parents Weekend—my mom, Sammy, and me. And speaking of your son, he had another great soccer game. He's our star goalie. He made three terrific saves in the game."

I sat in silence for awhile. The trees were in their full autumn colors, shivering and rustling in the occasional breeze. Red and yellow leaves floated down onto the graves.

Finally, I stood, walked over to place my hand atop Jonathan's headstone, whispered good-bye, and headed down the pathway toward my car. As always after visiting his grave, I felt a little better—and almost serene.

The feeling lasted through the drive to my office in the Central West End and up to the moment I stepped into the reception area of Gold & Brand, Attorneys At Law.

Chapter Thirteen

"My mother?"

Dorian, my assistant, nodded. "In your office."

I frowned. "Do you know why?"

Dorian smiled and shrugged. "She said she has a nice surprise for you."

Puzzled, I walked down the hall.

A nice surprise?

I paused in my office doorway. My mother was seated in one of the two chairs facing my desk, her head bowed as she read e-mails on her iPhone. She was wearing her workout outfit—a gray Johns Hopkins University sweatshirt, black stretch pants, and white tennis shoes. I smiled. According to what I've heard, among the older men who exercise at the Jewish Community Center, Sarah Gold is the redheaded Red Hot Mama of the fitness center. They flirt while she's on the hip abduction machine and vie for position on the treadmill next to hers. On more than one occasion my mother has remarked that there should be a special place in Hell for whoever invented Viagra. I try not to think about the implications of that statement.

"Mom?"

She turned toward me and smiled. "Hello, doll baby."

I came into my office, leaned over to give her a kiss, and took the seat next to hers.

"Is everything okay?"

Her smiled broadened. "Couldn't be better."

"Did you already exercise?"

"I'm heading there now. And then I'm having lunch with your client, Muriel."

I had represented my mother's friend Muriel Finkelstein and her neighborhood association in a crazy real estate case last year.

"Tell her hi," I said.

"I certainly will."

I gave her a look. "So?"

"You mean, so why am I here?"

"Yes, Mom."

She raised her eyebrows. "I have some very good news."

"Oh?"

"I'm coming from Max Kaminsky's office. That's why I'm dropping by. He's only six blocks away."

"Is everything okay?"

Dr. Kaminsky was her gynecologist.

"Couldn't be better. He said I have the uterus of a forty-year-old."

"That's nice, Mom."

"But that's not why I'm here. Guess who I met in his office?"

"Who?"

"Abe Rosen."

I frowned. The name wasn't familiar. "Who's that?"

"Who's that? I'll tell you. A nice Jewish boy, that's who. Better yet, a nice Jewish doctor. He just joined Max's practice."

"He's an ob/gyn?"

"He certainly is. Just moved here from Cincinnati. And he's no dummy. He's graduate of Yale Medical School. I saw his diploma. Not too shabby, Ms. Harvard Law School."

"Okay."

"And guess what else?"

I gave her a look. "What?"

She gave me a big wink. "He's not married."

"Okay."

"And?"

I sighed. "And what?"

"And guess who's coming to dinner tomorrow night?"

"Oh, my God, Mom. You didn't."

"I did. I told him I'd make him a nice brisket and my special chocolate babka."

"He's coming to dinner?"

"He certainly is."

"He's coming to my house?"

"At seven-thirty tomorrow. After Sammy is in bed. But don't worry. I'm taking care of dinner. Everything from soup to nuts. You'll be like a guest."

"I cannot believe this."

"You're going to like him, Rachel. I promise."

"I cannot believe this."

She stood and gave me a kiss on my forehead. "He's new to town. He doesn't know many people. Think of it as a mitzvah."

She paused at the door, turned back toward me, raised her eyebrows, and smiled. "A nice Jewish doctor."

She gave me another wink and left.

Chapter Fourteen

Golden Bough.

I smiled.

Of course.

But first, some background:

There are three things that make St. Louis unique:

The first is toasted ravioli, an appetizer you will find on the menu of every Italian restaurant and sports bar in town and almost nowhere else in the nation.

The second is the word "hoosier"—a term the rest of the nation understands as a proud nickname for an Indiana resident but in St. Louis is a derogatory term for a white-trash resident of the South City portion of St. Louis. Indeed, many a resident of our town is baffled when first learning that the Indiana University sports teams are known as, and are actually proud to be known as, the Hoosiers.

And the third thing unique to St. Louis is our obsession with our high school. As we natives know, the most common question posed when two locals meet is: "Where did you go to school?" And unlike residents of other cities, we understand that the term "school"—even when you're in a room filled with possessors of graduate and doctoral degrees—means high school. And we also know that the answer to that question will reveal a trove of sociological, cultural, and religious information that would make an anthropologist jealous.

The realm of St. Louis country clubs is as tiered and class-conscious as the realm of St. Louis high schools. And thus, when the conversation turns to golf or tennis among certain classes of men in our town, the inevitable question posed is, "Where do you belong?" If the one being asked that question had gone through a bris ceremony on the eighth day after his birth, his two most likely answers are "Briarcliff" or "Golden Bough."

My sister, Ann, and her husband, Richie, are members of Briarcliff, which to me is the worst of the worst: an exclusive *Jewish* country club—and thus a place where my people, victims of discrimination and exclusion throughout their history, can discriminate and exclude their own people. Founded more than a century ago by German-American Jews—including Richie's great-grandfather Hermann Marcus (née Chaim Marx)—Briarcliff strives for a *goyishe* version of Judaism, where corned beef is available only on St. Patrick's Day, lox is listed on the menu as smoked king salmon, the Friday night seafood buffet features a full array of shellfish, and the golf course is packed on Rosh Hashanah. As the men in their tennis whites sip their single malts on the veranda after a rousing game of doubles, they can pretend that they aren't stuck in a Yiddish minstrel version of a WASP country club.

But Golden Bough (a/k/a Goldenberg) has no such illusions. Founded by Eastern European Jews excluded from Briarcliff, it has become the proud land of pinky rings, Cadillac Escalades, high-roller junkets to Vegas, and bar mitzvah parties so lavish they could make a *Chasid* join Hezbollah. Among other dubious distinctions, Golden Bough has become the club of choice for the city's high-end divorce lawyers, many of whose clients are, ironically, members of St. Louis Country Club, Bellerive Country Club, and the other exclusive Gentile clubs that would grant a membership to a Jew just after they admitted a Martian. Nevertheless, the husbands in those Gentile clubs are convinced that when your divorce calls for an aggressive, brilliant, and ruthless lawyer, you need a Jew, and the best place to find one is at Golden Bough.

And thus Irving Sliman, former president of Golden Bough Country Club, came to represent Jerry Knight, membership committee chair of Laclede Country Club. That was seven years ago. Since then, Irving took up golf and retired, and Jerry took up a new wife and expired.

Irving Sliman looked up with a cold smile as the elderly maître d' pulled out the chair across the table from him and gestured for me to take a seat. He turned to Sliman with a slight bow.

"Your lunch companion has arrived, sir. This is Ms. Rachel Gold."

Sliman gave me a nod. "Hello, Rachel."

He turned to the maître d', held up his whiskey glass, and rattled the ice. "Philip, tell Roger to get me another Glenfiddich. I'm sure that the young lady would like something to drink as well. Send him over now."

The maître d' nodded gravely. "I will do that, sir."

While I never had a case against Irving Sliman during his years in practice, he had been such a presence in the St. Louis County Courthouse that the first time you saw him you could sense his authority. He'd been immediately recognizable: short, rail thin, bald, angular features, always clothed in an expensive navy or gray pinstriped suit, starched white shirt, dark bow tie, shiny black wingtips, and black horn-rimmed sunglasses, which he wore even indoors, although he'd set them on the podium when addressing the judge.

Now retired, his calendar was still managed by his longtime secretary, Gladys Parsons. I'd set up this meeting through Gladys, though Sliman chose the time and the forum.

He still had those horn-rimmed sunglasses, now pushed up onto his bald head, but he'd swapped out his bespoke suits and elegant bow ties for flashy golf attire, which today featured a shiny yellow shirt, white belt, and purple-and-pink plaid slacks. On someone else his age, the outfit would have seemed clownish. Not on Irving Sliman, though. With his prominent ears and the dark bags under his gray eyes, he reminded me of a ferret—a truly ominous ferret. Even his hoarse, low-pitched voice exuded menace.

An older black man in a tuxedo, presumably the Roger that Sliman had instructed the mâitre d' to summon, took our drink orders—another Glenfiddich on the rocks for Sliman, an iced tea with lemon for me. During the several minutes it took Roger to bring us our drinks, a procession of men of all ages stopped at our table to pay homage to Sliman, shaking his hand or patting him on the shoulder and saying how good it was to see him. It felt like a scene out of a *Godfather* movie. I recognized a state court judge, the managing partner of a major St. Louis law firm, a U.S. magistrate judge, a heart surgeon from Barnes-Jewish Hospital, and the head rabbi at one of the large reform synagogues.

Before his retirement, Irving Sliman had been the Sliman of The Sliman Law Firm, which, in addition to him, consisted of six paralegals, two contract lawyers (paid by the hour), and a registered nurse, all of whom handled the day-to-day tasks of his firm's lucrative plaintiff's personal injury practice. While Sliman tried the occasional lawsuit that didn't settle, he'd built an equally lucrative parallel practice representing wealthy St. Louisans— mostly men, but some women—in matters of particular interest to wealthy St. Louisans, which ranged from disputes with local public officials to disputes with their spouses. He had, over the years, become the *consigliore* to many of those men, providing trusted counsel on a variety of matters, legal and otherwise.

Although the nickname Slimeball seemed an irresistible moniker for an attorney named Sliman, its provenance was disputed. Some claimed its origins could be traced to the local insurance defense bar, whose exasperated attorneys had the unenviable task of trying to negotiate settlement agreements with Sliman. Others, however, claimed the nickname was a natural outgrowth of Sliman's second set of clients—the wealthy ones, many of whom sought him out because of his rumored con- nections to powerful public officials who, in response to a call from the Slimeball, would open governmental doors previously closed to those clients.

I fit into neither category. The goal of my meeting was a long shot, and my only angle was Sliman's son, Marc. His only child. Marc Sliman was now the Sliman of The Sliman Law Firm. But up until two years before his father's retirement, Marc Sliman had been a struggling worker's comp lawyer. In his late forties, Marc Sliman had been, in the jargon of the legal profession, a ham-and-egger. His father, however, had always protected him, and when it came time for the father to retire, the son stepped into the role of the Sliman of The Sliman Law Firm. The transition had been less than successful. My sources tell me the law firm is struggling. In particular, many of the firm's high-net-worth clients have moved on.

And thus the angle for my meeting.

Eventually, our drinks arrived and the supplicant pilgrimage ended.

"So," Sliman said in his low, raspy voice, pausing to take a sip of his drink, "you represent the former Mrs. Knight?"

"I do."

"I understand that you are not a lesbian, Miss Gold. Correct?"

I took sip of my iced tea and gazed at him. "Correct."

"So I can assume you are not fucking your client, if 'fucking' is the correct term of art for the sexual act between two dykes."

I took another sip of my iced tea and said nothing.

He smiled—or, rather, his facial muscles contorted his lips into something resembling a smile. "I understand the spoiled little snatch let it slip."

"Let what slip?"

"That your client was fucking her divorce lawyer."

"So she claimed."

"While under oath, eh?"

"She did." I took a sip of iced tea. "How did she know?"

Sliman shrugged. "I assume Jerry told her. Discretion was not Jerry's strong suit."

"And how did Jerry know?"

"Now, now, Counselor." He wagged his index finger at me. "Only the client can waive the attorney-client privilege, and that privilege remains alive even after the client dies. Thus until you can find me a reliable spiritualist who can communicate with my late client and obtain from him an unambiguous waiver of his privilege, my lips must remain sealed."

I smiled.

The waiter arrived, took our orders, and departed.

"You represented Jerry Knight," I said.

"I did, indeed."

"In more than just his divorce."

Sliman nodded. "He was a good client."

"And you represented his second wife, Danielle, right?"

"I did."

"More precisely, your law firm represented his second wife."

He nodded. "True."

"Until you retired."

"Until I retired."

"Your law firm no longer represents her."

"So it would seem."

"Did she explain why she took her legal business elsewhere?"

"You would need to direct that question toward a member of The Sliman Law Firm, of which I am no longer."

"And that member would be your son?"

Sliman took a sip of his drink and set the glass down on the table. "Are we playing Twenty Questions, young lady?"

"This is no game, Mr. Sliman."

"Please, call me Irving. I've dated women younger than you."

"Mazel tov."

He gave me what appeared to be a genuine smile. He raised his glass of Scotch toward me. "L'chaim."

I smiled. "L'chaim."

We clinked glasses.

The waiter arrived with our lunches—a slab of rare prime rib and an iceberg wedge with ranch dressing for Sliman, grilled fish tacos for me. Unbidden, the waiter returned with another Scotch on the rocks for Sliman and another iced tea with lemon for me.

We ate in silence for a few minutes.

Sliman wiped his chin with his cloth napkin. "So, is the subpoena in your purse or do you plan to serve it on my son?"

"The latter." Impressed, I checked my watch. "Just about now, I would assume. Which is why I wanted to meet with you."

"And why is that?"

"To assure you that I don't seek privileged communications between you and Mr. Knight, or between you and his second wife during the time you represented her. All I seek are communications between you and my client's former attorney. Those communications are not confidential, and my client is entitled to see them."

He nodded, cut another piece of his prime rib, and chewed it.

After a moment, he said, "I take it that the more direct route to those communications is not available."

"Correct."

He chuckled. "So Norma Cross destroyed the files."

"She claims her engagement letter gave her permission to do so."

"So she claims."

"I will deal with her and her claims later," I said. "I guarantee that."

He nodded. "Word on the street is that you don't fuck with Rachel Gold. I like that in a woman."

I smiled. "I've heard the same about you."

He shrugged. "I'm just a duffer these days with a ten handicap."

"As you know, Irving, Danielle Knight decided that The Sliman Law Firm wasn't good enough for her anymore. She took her business elsewhere. However, I'm assuming she didn't think to take her dead husband's files with her. When her fancy new law firm gets notice of the service of my subpoena on your old law firm, they are going to throw a hissy fit and do whatever they can to prevent your firm from producing anything from that file. That's why I asked for this meeting with you. Because your law firm's representation of Mr. Knight preceded your son's tenure at the firm, I wanted to give you this heads-up in the hopes that you can explain the situation to your son and assure him that the documents I seek are not confidential."

"Her lawyers will bring a motion for protective order," he said.

I nodded. "That's what I assume."

"Who is the judge?"

"Ballsack."

He smiled. "Harry, eh?"

"Yes."

"Nasty little prick." He took a sip of his whiskey and set down his glass. He gazed into my eyes, a hint of smile. "Harry won't be a problem for you here."

I smiled. "Thank you, Irving."

"As some wise man once said, 'What goes around comes around.' It's time little Danielle Knight learns that lesson."

Chapter Fifteen

The doorbell rang.

I glanced at the clock on the kitchen wall.

7:35 p.m.

I turned toward my mother, who gave me a beatific smile as she pressed the side of her index finger against her lips.

"I'll get the door," she whispered, and then raised her eyebrows. "You go upstairs, and I'll call you down."

I shook my head. "This isn't high school, Mom. I'm staying right here." I nodded toward the front door. "Go ahead. He's your guest."

"*Our* guest, doll baby." She paused to look me over, from head to toe. "You look absolutely gorgeous."

"The door, Mom."

"I'm going, I'm going."

I stood alone in the kitchen, bracing myself for the evening. Abe Rosen.

He sounded like a character in an episode of *Old Jews Telling Jokes.* In my mind he was short and bald, bushy gray eyebrows, bushy gray mustache. Except, according to my mother, this Abe Rosen was my age. A younger version of an old Jew, except not one telling jokes. More like one of those intense pre-med types from college. I flashed back to Harold Mishken from my freshman year—five feet three, eyes blurred behind the thick lenses of his black horn-rimmed glasses, a mouth-breather with halitosis. And now he was coming to my house for dinner.

Oy.

Come on, Rachel, I told myself. *Be a mensch. This wasn't his idea. Who knows what my mother told him about me? The poor guy is probably a nervous wreck. Be nice to him.*

I heard the door open.

"Oh, my goodness, Doctor," my mother said. "Those are beautiful. Oh, and wine, too. Such a sweetie."

A pause.

"Oh, Rachel," she yodeled, as if she were Julie Andrews singing "The Lonely Goatherd" from *The Sound of Music,* "our guest has arrived."

I took a deep breath, exhaled, and stepped out of the kitchen.

"Here she is. Dr. Rosen, my wonderful daughter, Rachel. Rachel, this is Dr. Rosen."

As you probably figured out already, this was not the Abe Rosen I expected. Not even close. This version was tall—maybe six feet four. This version was trim and athletic. And blond and hazel-eyed. And handsome. Hollywood handsome. Maybe not leading-man handsome, but sexy sidekick handsome.

He stepped toward me and held out his hand. "Hello, Rachel. I'm Abe."

We shook. "Hi."

He was casually dressed—blue chambray shirt, sleeves rolled up, khaki slacks, brown loafers. Neat, but not too coiffed, which for me is a deal killer.

"Look at these flowers," my mother said. "And a bottle of wine, too. The good stuff. Not Mogen David."

"My pleasure, Mrs. Gold. It was sweet of you to invite me to dinner."

◇◇◇

Dinner was a delight.

Abe was charming and funny, and he was genuinely appreciative of being invited for dinner. As for the meal itself, my mother served up a Michelin Three-star version of her greatest Ashkenazi hits, which featured beet borscht with a dollop of sour cream, chopped liver with toasted challah, brisket, oven-roasted red potatoes, and sautéed French green beans.

In response to my mother's nearly nonstop series of questions, I learned that Abe had grown up in Cincinnati and gone to Miami of Ohio, where he'd played forward on the varsity basketball team the year they'd reached the Sweet Sixteen before losing to Duke. From there he went to medical school at Yale and then a residency at the Cleveland Clinic, where he met his future wife, Sheila Bronson, who was doing her residency in plastic surgery. The two young doctors married, settled in Cincinnati, had two kids—both girls, now five and eight—and then, a year ago, divorced. His ex-wife Sheila, who'd grown up in St. Louis, wanted to move back home with the children to be near her parents. (Turns out she was three years ahead of me at Clayton, our rival high school. I didn't know her, but, this being St. Louis, I knew her younger brother, Robby.) Wanting to stay close to his daughters, Abe moved to St. Louis, too, arriving a month ago.

Between dinner and dessert, Abe and I had a chance to talk a little more privately as my mother rattled around in the kitchen, insisting that we remain at the table.

He leaned toward me and, in a soft voice, said, "She's quite a character, your mom."

I nodded. "That she is."

"She's terrific. I hope this hasn't been too awkward for you."

"Actually," I said with a smile, "it's been a pleasure."

He smiled, too. "Same here."

"That's good to hear. I can't imagine what she told you about me."

"Very low key. Just that you were—let's see—an honors graduate of Harvard Law School, an esteemed trial attorney, and still as beautiful as when you were the captain of the cheerleader squad in high school."

"Oy."

"Believe me, Rachel, if it had been my mother describing me to you, you'd think I was on the cusp of winning the Nobel

Prize in Medicine, having turned down a Hall-of-Fame career in the NBA."

I laughed. "It must be one of the requirements to get certified as a Jewish mother."

"What's this about getting certified?" my mother asked.

She was standing in the doorway with her chocolate babka on a serving plate.

"Just joking, Mom. What can we do to help?"

"I have tea brewing in the kitchen."

I stood. "I'll get the teacups."

"I have a plate with sliced lemons."

"I'll bring them in, too."

Abe stood. "I'll get the dessert plates."

The babka was, of course, delicious. Like so many of my mother's dishes, it came from a recipe her mother brought to America from Lithuania. Not a written recipe, of course. My grandmother had learned to cook from her mother and her aunts and her grandmothers in the crowded family kitchen in Vilna. After my grandmother was diagnosed with cancer, my mother spent hours in the kitchen cooking with her, watching carefully, measuring everything, and writing down the recipes, copies of which she gave to Ann and me. I've tried to make her babka. My version isn't bad, but it's nothing like my mother's.

"Rachel has a case right up your alley," my mother said.

"Mom." I shook my head. "Abe's not here to talk about lawsuits."

"A medical malpractice case?" he asked.

"Absolutely not," I said. "Don't worry, Abe. I don't do med mal."

"Tell him," my mother said. "She's representing a widow whose husband got her pregnant. But only after was dead. Crazy, eh? Only in America."

"It's not that crazy," I said. "She was impregnated with his sperm, which had been frozen and stored long before he died."

"What's the issue in the lawsuit?" he asked.

"Under her husband's will, the little girl will inherit a fortune if she is in his bloodline. The son from his first marriage is challenging her inheritance."

"On what ground?"

"That she isn't his child."

"Based on what?"

"Originally, it was based on the little girl's birth date. She was born eleven months after the husband's death."

"But you said the mother got pregnant from a frozen sperm deposit."

"Exactly. The son didn't know that when he filed the lawsuit."

"And now?"

"I'm hoping to end the lawsuit tomorrow."

"How?"

"I'm taking the deposition of the custodian of the records at the sperm bank."

"Which sperm bank?"

"Procreative Cryogenics. Their St. Louis office."

He nodded. "They have an excellent reputation."

"That's good to hear."

"I worked with their Cincinnati office for two patients of mine whose husbands were sterile. The donors, though, were anonymous."

"Fortunately, this donor wasn't. If all goes well tomorrow, the case will be over."

Famous last words.

Chapter Sixteen

The deposition took place in my conference room. I had served the subpoena on the St. Louis office of Procreative Cryogenics seeking all records regarding Bert Mulligan's sperm deposits. Although Cyndi no longer had the access number assigned to the vials of frozen sperm, you only needed that number if you wanted access to those vials, which no longer existed. Cyndi had used all five vials in getting pregnant with Carson. But since we only needed the records regarding those sperm deposits, I confirmed in advance with the company's lawyer that the donor's full name and Social Security number would be sufficient.

The witness for Procreative Cryogenics was George Luntz, a rail-thin middle-aged man in a white short-sleeved shirt, pencil mustache, and red bow tie. Also present were Bert Grimsley; Bert's lawyer, Milton Strauss; and the company's lawyer, a young male partner from Thompson Coburn whose name I've already forgotten.

The deposition lasted less than thirty minutes. After the court reporter swore in the witness, I asked Mr. Luntz the usual pre-liminaries—name, address, job title, job responsibilities—and then got to the point:

Gold: Mr. Luntz, I am handing you what the court reporter has marked as Defendant's Exhibit A. Do you recognize it?

Luntz: Yes, ma'am.

Gold:	Is that the subpoena served on your company, Procreative Cryogenics, LLC?
Luntz:	Yes, ma'am.
Gold:	Near the bottom of the first page of Defendant's Exhibit A is a description of the documents you are required to bring to the deposition today. Correct?
Luntz:	Yes, ma'am.
Gold:	The documents sought by the subpoena consist of all of your company's records for sperm deposits made by one Bertram James Mulligan, correct?
Luntz:	Yes, ma'am.
Gold:	The subpoena further identifies Mr. Mulligan by his Social Security number, correct?
Luntz:	Yes, ma'am.
Gold:	Are a sperm donor's name and Social Security number among the information used as identifiers for persons making sperm deposits with your company?
Luntz:	Yes, ma'am.
Gold:	Very good, sir. What documents have you brought with you today?
Luntz:	Well, I don't have any with me.
Gold:	What do you mean?
Luntz:	I did not bring any with me.
Gold:	Why not?
Luntz:	Well, you see, we don't have any, ma'am.

Gold:	Please explain.
Luntz:	We searched our files. We have no record of any transaction, sperm or otherwise, with that gentlemen.
Gold:	(Pause) You have nothing?
Luntz:	Nothing.
Gold:	No documents at all?
Luntz:	None, ma'am.
Gold:	Nothing under that Social Security number?
Luntz:	No, ma'am.
Gold:	(Pause) I have no further questions.
Strauss:	(Laughs) I guess I have a few follow-ups for you, Mr. Luntz. You're saying you have no such records, eh?
Luntz:	We have nothing under that Social Security number.
Strauss:	Do you have any reason to believe that the number is wrong?
Luntz:	No, sir.
Strauss:	Does your company always obtain names and Social Security numbers for folks storing their sperm with you?
Luntz:	To the best of my knowledge, yes.
Strauss:	Any other ID numbers for them?
Luntz:	The specific vials of sperm will be given an access code.
Strauss:	Were there any access codes associated with the late Mr. Mulligan?

Luntz:	Not to my knowledge. That code would ordinarily be included with the other identification numbers.
Strauss:	And it's not like the late Mr. Mulligan was just some Joe Blow off the street, right?
Luntz:	I'm sorry, sir. I'm not following you.
Strauss:	You know who he was, right?
Luntz:	I never personally met him.
Strauss:	But you know he was CEO and chairman of The Mulligan Group, right?
Luntz:	That's my understanding, sir.
Strauss:	And The Mulligan Group, well, those folks own your company, right?
Luntz:	I believe so, sir.
Strauss:	So when you get a subpoena asking for information about the former CEO and chairman of The Mulligan Group, you're going to do an extra careful search, right?
Luntz:	We do a careful search in response to every subpoena, sir.
Strauss:	And you did that careful search here?
Luntz:	Yes, sir.
Strauss:	That's all I got. Counsel, he's all yours.
Gold:	No further questions.
Grimsley:	Well, lady, looks to me like that lying bitch snookered you good. You *and* my father. You're all toast. You better warn that gold digger—

Strauss:	—Whoa, Bert. This depo is over. We're off the record now.
Gold:	No, we are still on the record. And so is this, Mr. Strauss. Get your obnoxious client out of my office immediately or I'm calling Judge Bauer.

◇◇◇

"Maybe he's right," Benny said. "Maybe you did get snookered."

I shook my head. "I believe her, Benny. Cyndi knew I was going to serve that subpoena. She was excited. She couldn't wait to get the records. We both thought it would end the case."

We were in my office. Benny had dropped by after a faculty meeting to go to lunch. He found me seated at my desk and staring at the ceiling.

"Have you told her?"

I nodded. "I called her. After they left."

"What'd she say?"

"It doesn't make sense to her." I sighed. "Or to me."

"You think someone's screwed with the records? Maybe hacked their computer?"

"It's possible, I suppose. Something is definitely off."

"When's the trial?"

"A week from next Monday."

"Holy shit, woman. What are you going to do?"

"Good question."

"You'll figure something out."

"I hope so."

"You always do. What about your other zombie case? The one where you have the first wife instead of the trophy one?"

I smiled. "Another hearing. Tomorrow morning."

"In front of old Hairy Balls?"

"Ballsack. And remember: if you ever appear before him you had better pronounce his last name like the French author. Balzac—as in 'zack,' not 'sack.' Otherwise, he gets even nastier than normal."

"What's this hearing about?"

I raised my eyebrows. "It should be interesting."

Benny grinned. "Oh?"

"I served a document subpoena on Jerry Knight's divorce lawyer. Actually, on his law firm. Irving Sliman was his lawyer, but he's retired. His son runs the firm. The subpoena asks for all non-privileged documents from Jerry Knight's divorce file."

"So what's in court?"

"The second wife—Danielle—filed an objection to the subpoena."

"On what grounds?"

"A whole grab bag—invasion of privacy, abuse of discovery, irrelevance."

"What about Sliman's law firm? They were the dead man's attorneys."

"No objection from them."

"Really?"

"I actually met with Irving before I served the subpoena. I explained it to him. He's okay."

"No shit? You telling me that in his retirement Slimeball has turned into Elmo?"

"Hardly. I was hoping that there'd be a personal angle for him, and maybe there is. His son is definitely not a chip off the old block. Rumors are that the law firm is struggling. Jerry Knight was a good client of Irving's, and when he died there were lots of matters that Irving was handling. I think the son is angry that Danielle yanked her business from his firm after Irving retired. I'm hoping I've hit a nerve."

Benny chuckled. "Nicely played."

"Maybe. We'll see. Irving even indicated he might—just might—put in a call to Ballsack before the hearing tomorrow."

"What goes around comes around, eh?"

"His words exactly."

"Beautiful. But enough of this law shit. Let's eat, woman. I'm starving."

Chapter Seventeen

As we approached the podium, Judge Ballsack leaned back in his chair, crossed his arms over his chest, and shook his head in annoyance.

"Here again, eh?" he said in his high-pitched, nasal voice

"But this time, Your Honor," I said, "Mr. Sterling seems to believe that he does have a dog in the fight."

"That we do, Judge," Tom Sterling said.

"Hold your horses, Mr. Sterling—or your dogs or elephants or whatever. I'd like to first hear from the real party in interest here. Mr. Sliman?"

Marc Sliman cleared his throat. "Yes, Your Honor."

Judge Ballsack held up the court papers. "This subpoena was served on your firm, *not* on Mr. Sterling's. It seeks documents from your firm, *not* from Mr. Sterling's. It seeks documents from the file of your client, *not* Mr. Sterling's. To use Mr. Sterling's hoosier metaphor, if anyone's got a dog in this fight, it's you."

Marc Sliman nodded. "Certainly more than Mr. Sterling, Your Honor."

"However," Judge Ballsack said, cupping his hand over his ear, "I am not hearing you barking."

Sliman shrugged and grinned. To state that he looked nothing like his father was to state the obvious. Marc Sliman was pudgy, slightly bucktoothed, and wore his thinning black hair in a comb-over. His gray suit looked two sizes two large, his dress shirt was wrinkled, and his thick-soled black shoes needed a shine.

"Well?" Ballsack said, leaning forward, hand still cupped over his ear. "Are you going to bark for us?"

Sliman shook his head. "No, Your Honor. Ms. Gold's subpoena makes it clear that she does not seek any privileged communications between my law firm and the late Mr. Knight. Thus we have no objection."

Ballsack turned to Tom Sterling. "Well, Mr. Sterling, as they say out in Hollywood, that's a wrap. Your objection is overruled."

"Your Honor," Sterling said, "before you overrule my objections, and I have more than one, I'd like to point out a few things of concern to my client. The first issue is that—"

"—Sterling," the judge snapped, his face red, "clean the wax out of your redneck ears. I have read your papers and I have overruled your objections, and thus whatever you claim you would like to point out is now moot."

The judge turned to me. "Draft an order denying the objections, young lady, and give it to my clerk.

I nodded. "Thank you, Your Honor."

"Wait." He was looking beyond the podium, frowning. "Miss Cross?"

I turned. Norma Cross was seated in the second row in the gallery. She stood. "Yes?"

"Approach the bench," the judge said.

She did.

"What are you doing in my courtroom?"

She gazed up at him with her attempt at an innocent smile. "Oh, I just happened to be in the courthouse on another matter and decided to drop in."

He stared down at her. "Why is that?"

She shrugged. "Curiosity."

"About this case?"

"Yes. As the Court will recall, my firm's records were the subject of a prior subpoena by Miss Gold."

"Yes, indeed. As I recall, that subpoena sought highly relevant documents in this case that your firm conveniently destroyed, correct?"

"That subpoena sought client files that had been destroyed in the ordinary course of business and with the client's express permission, as stated in the engagement letter."

"That's what she said." The judge leaned back in his chair. "What exactly are you afraid of, Miss Cross?"

She gave him another smile. "In this case? With this lawyer?" She nodded toward me and chuckled. "Absolutely nothing."

There was a long moment of silence as the two stared at one another.

The judge nodded. "Just curiosity?"

"Exactly."

"They say it killed the cat. Be careful out there." And then the judge banged his gavel. "Next case!"

Chapter Eighteen

Although nearly three million people live in the St. Louis metropolitan area, it's still a small town for us Jews. We typically are just two degrees of separation from every other Jew in the area. If you know someone Jewish who is from St. Louis, ask me the next time you see me. Odds are I know him or her, or at least someone in that family.

Which is why I was having coffee and banana-blueberry bread with Abe Rosen at the Osage Café in the Central West End that Saturday morning. In addition to his connection to my mother via Dr. Kaminsky, I discovered that his ex-wife, Sheila (the one whose brother I know), and I were members of Central Reform Congregation, and thus my son, Sam, and her two daughters, Sofia and Madeline, attended religious school there every Saturday. Sam and Sofia, as I learned that morning, were actually in the same class.

Abe had the girls for the weekend, and when he called on Friday to see whether I'd be free for coffee on Saturday after I dropped Sam off at religious school, it was—as my mother would say, and actually did say, and more than once—*beshert*, which is Yiddish for "meant to be."

Keep it casual, I reminded myself on the way over to Osage Café. *No business.*

It was tempting, especially given his medical specialty, to ask him questions about the missing sperm donor records in my crazy paternity case for Cyndi Mulligan. But I had agreed to have coffee with Abe to get better acquainted and not to evaluate a prospective expert witness on artificial insemination issues. Fortunately, I'd spoken with a family-law lawyer earlier in the week, and he'd given me some good advice for my next move in Cyndi's case.

Abe was already there when I arrived, and as he stood to greet me I was once again taken by his looks. He was the blond version of tall, dark, and handsome, dressed today in faded jeans, a black T-shirt, and running shoes. He was apparently not on call, since he hadn't shaved that morning, which added a scruffy (i.e., sexy) touch to his appearance.

We talked baseball and food and music—each of which we both loved, though our tastes differed. As for baseball, he was, alas, a Reds fan—an understandable affliction traceable to his place of birth. As for food, my favorite restaurants were Thai and Indian while his were barbecue (Memphis style) and Greek. He was convinced that there was a gyro food truck up on Mount Olympus. As for music, I loved Tom Petty and Frank Sinatra while he preferred Bruce Springsteen and Willie Nelson. But with the exception of the Reds, these were differences of opinion I could tolerate—and even enjoy.

"Jonathan was a Willie Nelson fan," I said, "and, believe it or not, he was also a Johnny Cash fan, a Merle Haggard fan, and a huge Doc Watson fan. Never figured out how a nice Jewish boy from Brooklyn—a nice *Orthodox* Jewish boy—ended up such a big country music fan."

"Maybe his cantor sang with a twang," Abe said.

I smiled. "You might be right. A few years back, I was in a case with a Jewish lawyer from Alabama. He told me that when he was in Israel he went to Saturday morning services at a synagogue in Tel Aviv. They called him up to the *bimah* to recite the Torah blessings. He did it all in Hebrew—never said a word of English. Afterward, one of the congregants asked him what part of the South he was from. He asked the man how he knew. 'Easy,' the man said. 'Your accent.'"

Abe laughed. "Nice."

His smile faded. He took a sip of coffee and gazed at me. "How long has he been dead, Rachel?"

"It'll be three years this fall."

He nodded, his eyes sad. "Your mom told me you've raised his two daughters."

"My mom was a big help." I smiled. "They're wonderful girls. They call her Baba. They adore her."

"Your mom says they adore you."

"I do love them, and my heart goes out to them. To lose your mother when you're just a child, and then your father." I shook my head. "I can't imagine."

"I can't either. Though it's not nearly the same, my father died during the summer after I graduated from high school. A heart attack. He'd been so excited about my basketball scholarship. The week after I accepted the offer from Miami of Ohio he bought season tickets, even though I told him I'd probably spend most of that first year sitting on the bench. He didn't care. He was so proud. He was planning to drive down to Oxford for every home game. He even made me a blown-up copy of the seating chart at Millet Hall—that's their basketball arena—so that I'd know where he'd be sitting. He placed a red circle around his seat."

He paused and took a sip of coffee. "Whenever I got in a game that year, I'd glance over to that empty seat." He shrugged. "You eventually get over the pain of your loss, but you never stop missing them."

I nodded, thinking of my late father, and of Jonathan.

He gave me a sheepish smile and shook his head. "Boy, this conversation has sure taken a cheerful turn."

"Well, on a lighter note, my mother was so proud when she came home from her annual exam with your partner."

"Oh?"

"He apparently told her that she had the uterus of a forty-year-old."

He laughed and raised his coffee mug toward me. "Mazel tov to Sarah Gold."

We clinked mugs.

The waitress arrived with a pot of coffee. "Care for more?"

I checked my watch. "Whoa. We need to get back." I looked up at the waitress. "We better get our bill."

She smiled. "It's already been taken care of."

I turned to Abe. "Really?"

"My pleasure. You're a cheap date."

"My turn next time."

"Deal."

We shook hands in the parking lot.

"This was nice, Rachel."

"I had fun. Take care."

"You, too."

Chapter Nineteen

Throughout the first year of the divorce proceeding captioned *In re the Marriage of Jerome R. Knight and Marsha B. Knight*, Adam Fox personified a Cross Law Firm lawyer. In his role as Marsha Knight's attorney, he was every bit as aggressive, uncooperative, obnoxious, and underhanded as his firm's namesake, Norma Cross.

Until suddenly he wasn't.

All was revealed in the hundreds of documents comprising the case file that I reviewed in a conference room at The Sliman Law Firm. Irving's son, Marc, had met me in the lobby and escorted me to the conference room, where three cardboard storage boxes of documents awaited. Marc explained that he'd gone through the files and had removed just one folder on the ground that its contents were protected from disclosure under the attorney work product privilege. That folder was labeled "Trial Strategy" and contained, he explained, his father's notes on potential trial exhibits, cross-examinations, and the like. Given that the case had settled before trial, I wasn't that concerned about those documents.

Reviewing the case file in a typical lawsuit—even a divorce case—can be a tedious, yawn-producing task. First comes the initial written discovery—the interrogatories and document requests written in eye-numbing legalese—which are followed by written objections to those written discovery requests, which are followed by negotiations over those objections, sometimes via correspondence, other times by telephone followed by correspondence confirming those negotiations, which are followed by supplemental partial answers to the written discovery requests, which are followed by more negotiations over the inadequacies of the answers, which are followed by a motion to compel more responsive answers, and so on and so on.

But not so with the case file for *In re the Marriage of Jerome R. Knight and Marsha B. Knight*. Oh, there were interrogatories and there were letters and there were motions, but not of the usual versions. The divorce case was filed in February. The first sign of trouble came in May in the form of a four-page letter from Adam Fox to Irving Sliman that began: "This will confirm the agreements we reached today during our discussion of your client's meritless objections to my client's interrogatories and request for production of documents."

Irving Sliman's response, two days later, opened: "Unless you were smoking crack cocaine during our discovery conference or were otherwise under the influence of a hallucinogen, young man, there is no excuse for the outrageous misrepresentations contained in your letter. What you purport to confirm is nothing more than a slapdash and scurrilous pack of mendacities."

And things went downhill from there. They were in court three times over discovery disputes that first year—and the transcripts from those three hearings were, to put it mildly, incendiary. During the third hearing, Irving Sliman announced to the Court that from that point forward he would no longer engage in a conversation with Adam Fox without a witness. Specifically, as he stated, he would have his secretary, Gladys Parsons, present or listening in on every conversation with Mr. Fox and transcribing the entirety of each one.

And so she did. A folder labeled "Transcriptions" contained transcripts of more than a dozen telephone conversations, including one—a dispute over scheduling the deposition of Marsha Knight—that ended up as Exhibit A to Sliman's motion to compel that deposition.

That first year of the lawsuit was the litigation equivalent of a mud-wrestling match with the trial judge in the role of referee.

Adam Fox received far more penalties than Irving Sliman that year. The mud-wrestling continued into the early months of the second year of the lawsuit. By the time my document review had reached the fourth month of that second year, however, I had gone through all the files in the first two boxes of documents and was almost two-thirds of the way through the last box. Obviously, something was about to happen.

The first indication came on September 28th in the form of an e-mail that Irving Sliman's secretary, Gladys Parsons, sent to Adam Fox at 10:47 a.m. Irving apparently didn't use a computer and didn't have e-mail. It read:

> Mr. Sliman requests a meeting with you to discuss an important matter. Are you available tomorrow afternoon at 3 p.m.? He will meet you in the 14th floor lounge at the St. Louis Club?

Fox responded at 11:21:

> Yes, I am available. Who else will be attending? And exactly what is the nature of this purported "important matter"?

Her response, sent at 11:28:

> The attendees will be just you and Mr. Sliman. As for the nature of the matter, Mr. Sliman will explain that in full at the meeting.

And then six weeks of silence until the following e-mail from Irving Sliman's secretary to Adam Fox on November 5th:

> Attached for your review is the real estate deed that Mr. Knight's LLC is prepared to execute in connection with the divorce settlement.

Attached to that e-mail was a draft of the real estate deed. I reviewed it. With just minor modifications, it was the version of the deed for the apartment complex that was at the heart of Jerry Knight's widow's lawsuit against Marsha Knight.

That was the last e-mail to Adam Fox.

The only other communication with him in the file was the transcript a telephone conversation eight days after that November 5th e-mail—the one that had included as an attachment the draft real estate deed:

Call commenced: 2:02 pm

Mr. S: What's the problem now, Fox?

Fox: You know exactly what it is.

Mr. S: Cut to the chase, son. What's the problem?

Fox: That deed you sent me. That's the problem.

Mr. S: I don't see any problem with that deed. The instrument accomplishes precisely what it is intended to accomplish.

Fox: Come on, Sliman. What you apparently intend to accomplish is not exactly consistent with my client's interests.

Mr. S: I represent my client, not yours.

Fox: I can't believe this.

Mr. S: You can't believe what?

Fox: This isn't right.

Mr. S: I disagree.

Fox: Come on. My concern is easy to resolve.

Mr. S: Oh, really? How so?

Fox: Make it a trust. I checked.

Mr. S: You checked what?

Fox: Chapter 456 of the Missouri Revised Statutes. Section 456.025. It solves the issue.

Mr. S:	I hardly think so.
Fox:	What do you mean?
Mr. S:	My draft solves the issue. I checked the rules.
Fox:	You checked what?
Mr. S:	Come on, Adam. We play by the rules.
Fox:	You mean 4-1.8? Come on, Irving. This is bullshit.
Mr. S:	Your issue, not mine. My client has approved the draft. Get your client's consent and we're done.
Fox:	This is bullshit.
Mr. S:	Get her to consent to the deed, Fox. You have until Friday to send me the signed consent.

Call ended: 2:13 pm.

◇◇◇

Marsha Knight's signed consent arrived two days later, and twenty-three days after that the court entered the divorce decree.

The final document in the file was a printout of an e-mail exchange between Sliman's secretary and Norma Cross. The e-mails were dated March 9th of the following year—about three months after entry of the divorce decree.

To:	Norma Cross
From:	Gladys Parsons on behalf of Irving Sliman
Subject:	In re Marriage of Knight

Mr. Sliman requests a meeting with you to discuss an important matter. Are you available tomorrow afternoon at 2 p.m.? He will meet you in the 14th floor lounge at the St. Louis Club?

To: Gladys Parson

From: Norma Cross

Subject: RE: In re Marriage of Knight

He's mistaken. This was Adam's case.

To: Norma Cross

From: Gladys Parsons on behalf of Irving Sliman

Subject: RE: In re Marriage of Knight

Mr. Sliman is not mistaken. He requests only you. It will be strictly private.

To which Norma responded with one word:

Okay.

And that was the last document in the last box of The Sliman Law Firm's case file for *In re the Marriage of Jerome R. Knight and Marsha B. Knight.*

Chapter Twenty

My cell phone buzzed just as our waitress set down our drinks—an iced tea for me, a draft beer for Benny. I read the text message.

"Jacki?" Benny asked.

I nodded. "Just got out of court. Be here in ten minutes."

The waitress said, "Can I get you two something while you wait?"

I looked at Benny. "Your call."

He looked up at the waitress. "I'm having a powerful yearning for chicken wings." He glanced over at me. "Okay?"

I shrugged. "Fine."

"Dry, mild, or hot?" she asked.

Benny gave her a wink. "Hotter the better."

She smiled and nodded as she wrote it down. "Extra hot."

"And make it a large."

I looked down at the menu. "Benny, large is two pounds of wings."

"To quote Immanuel Kant, 'You can never have enough chicken wings.'"

The waitress looked at Benny and then at me. "So a large?"

I sighed. "A large."

After she left, I looked at Benny. "I can't believe you."

"It's an appetizer."

"You call two pounds of wings an appetizer?"

"Just a *forshbeiz*. Something to hold me over until Jacki gets here." He took a sip of beer, looked at me, shook his head, and sighed. "Ah, Rachel."

"What?"

"You have many awesome qualities: killer legs, great courtroom skills, all-world tush, a deeper knowledge of baseball than most men. But you also have a tragic flaw."

"Which is?"

"Your blasé attitude toward chicken wings. Frankly, I don't understand. We're talking about one of the greatest inventions of the twentieth century, right up there with the airplane, the computer, and Internet porn."

"I'm just not a fan."

He shook his head. "It boggles the mind."

The waitress arrived with a huge, steaming platter of wings. "Here we go, kids. Enjoy!"

I watched as Benny dug in. After three wings, he wiped his chin, took a big gulp of beer, and smiled at me. "Nu?"

I frowned. "Nu?"

He gave me a wink. "Abe Rosen, eh?"

"You'd like him, Benny."

"Your mom sure does."

"Oh, my God. My mother? Don't get me started. I met him for coffee last Saturday morning, and now she's ready to hire a wedding planner."

"What did you expect? He's every Jewish mother's dream: a nice Jewish doctor."

I swatted my hand in the air. "Next topic."

Benny finished another wing. "How's that zombie case coming?"

"Which zombie case?"

"The one with the widow whose husband mysteriously schtupped her from the grave."

"That would be Cyndi Mulligan."

"Right. Last time we talked, you'd learned that the sperm bank had no records of her husband's alleged sperm deposits. Which means—what was her husband's name?"

"Bert Mulligan."

92 *Michael A. Kahn*

"Right. That means if Bert ain't the daddy, Cyndi's kid inherits *bupkis* and that creepy son from his first marriage—what did that asshole change his name to?"

"Grimsley. Formerly Bert Mulligan, Junior. Now Bert Grimsley."

"Grimsley. Right. So if Cyndi loses, the Grim Reaper inherits the dead man's company. Right?"

I nodded. "That's pretty much the scenario."

"Scenario? I believe the correct legal term is clusterfuck."

"Probably."

Benny gave me a wink. "So?"

"So?"

"To paraphrase Johnny from *Dirty Dancing*: Nobody puts Rachel in the corner. Let's hear your Plan B for beating the Grim Reaper."

I smiled. "This is a paternity case, right?"

"Right."

"What would you normally do in a paternity case?"

"Have the alleged father submit to one of those DNA tests."

"Exactly."

"Are you shitting me? You're going to actually dig up old Bert?"

"No. Cyndi doesn't want that, and, frankly, neither do I. I'd need to get a court order to have him disinterred, and then Grimsley would know what I was doing. That's way too risky."

"Why too risky?"

I raised my eyebrows. "Benny..."

"What?"

"It's too risky because I don't know how a paternity test would come out. I believe Cyndi, Benny. I really do. But I wasn't born yesterday. I can't eliminate the possibility that Bert Mulligan isn't the father. And that's one of only two possible outcomes of a paternity test—and probably the more likely of the two."

"So what are you going to do?"

"I talked to a family law lawyer. Turns out that many of these genetic testing outfits offer more than just paternity tests. They have various kinship tests. The results aren't as definitive as a paternity test, but depending on the DNA analysis they will be able to say, for example, that the potential uncle is ten times more likely to be the actual uncle than to be just some unrelated guy. Keep in mind that Grimsley has the burden of proof. He has to prove that Bert Mulligan *isn't* the father. If I can get an expert to testify that it's more likely than not that Bert Mulligan *is* the father, how is Grimsley going to refute that?"

"Assuming you can get an expert to testify to that."

"Right."

He munched on another wing and washed it down with a gulp of beer.

"Do you have a potential uncle?" he asked.

"Not above ground. Cyndi has a copy of Bert's family records. We went through them yesterday. He had an older brother and a younger sister. They're both dead. The brother never married, but the sister did, and she had a daughter."

"Still alive?"

I nodded. "Barb. She lives in Omaha. I spoke with her this morning. Nice gal. I explained the situation. She agreed to participate."

"What does she have to do?"

"Not much. The DNA testing outfit has an office in Omaha. They're going to send someone over tomorrow morning to get a cheek swab. That's all they need from her. They're getting some blood from Cyndi's daughter today. The added bonus is that it'll all be confidential. If the test results are bad, well, Grimsley will never know."

"When will you have the results?"

"Next Thursday."

"Next Thursday. And the trial is the following Monday." Benny shook his head. "Cutting it close, woman, especially if you're doing this trial all on your own."

I smiled. "As I recall, you don't teach class on Mondays, Professor."

He grinned. "You are correct, Ms. Gold. I try to reserve my Mondays for drilling new assholes in creepy litigants."

I held up my glass of iced tea and tilted toward him "Then there just may be a role for you in court that day."

We clinked our glasses.

"You're adding this wild man to your trial team?"

We both looked up. Jacki was standing at the head of our booth.

She looked down at Benny. "Scoot over, stud."

Benny grinned and slid down the bench toward the wall.

"Help yourself, sexy." He gestured toward the platter of wings. "I ordered them with you in mind."

Jacki's eyes widened. "Whoa." She turned to Benny and placed a hand over her heart. "A wild man, yes, but also my hero."

Chapter Twenty-one

After the waitress set down our lunches—a chef salad for Jackie; a cup of gazpacho and a grilled cheese sandwich for me; a cheeseburger, fries, onion rings, and an order of fried cheddar cheese balls for Benny—we got down to business, namely, the other zombie case, a/k/a Marsha Knight's Rule Against Perpetuities battle with her ex-husband's second wife, Danielle.

"You're helping Rachel on that one, right?" Benny asked.

Jacki nodded. "I got dibs on Norma Cross."

"Who makes a cameo appearance," I said, "in the very last document in the Sliman case file."

"That e-mail asking her to meet Sliman, right?" Jacki said.

I nodded. "Three months after the case was over."

"That's some weird shit," Benny said.

Jacki turned to me. "Did you figure out those cites in that last conversation between Sliman and Adam Fox?"

"The first one was easy. The second one, though—" I smiled. "Intriguing."

"How so?" Jacki asked.

I unzipped my briefcase and took out three copies of the last page of the transcript of that telephone conversation. I handed one copy to Benny and one to Jackie.

"So they're talking about Sliman's draft of that real estate deed," I said, pointing to where that part of the conversation started. "The version that violates the Rule Against Perpetuities.

Adam Fox says he's found the solution. Make it a trust, he says. He's checked. Checked what, Sliman asks? Fox answers, Section 456.025. It solves the issues."

"So what is that?" Benny asked.

"The Missouri legislature's solution to avoid the Rule Against Perpetuities. I had to read it a few times to figure it out."

"So you need a trust?" Jacki asked.

"Exactly." I took out my notes. "The statute says, and I quote, 'The Rule Against Perpetuities shall not apply to a trust if the trustee has the power to sell the trust property during the period of time that the trust continues beyond the period of the Rule Against Perpetuities that would apply to the trust but for this statute.'"

"In English, please," Benny said.

"So long as you put the property in a trust, you can have a crazy time frame and a crazy inheritance scheme that would otherwise be invalid."

"But Sliman refused to do it," Jacki said.

Benny frowned. "So Adam Fox knew at the time of that call that the deed was probably invalid under the Rule Against Perpetuities."

I nodded. "It seems so."

Benny chewed on an onion ring. "But he let his client go forward anyway."

"Yep."

"Sounds like malpractice to me," Benny said. "Why would he do that?"

I pointed at the transcript. "Look at what Sliman says. He rejects the idea of a trust and says, 'My draft solves the issue.' He says, 'I checked.' Adam Fox asks what he checked. And Sliman says 'Come on, Adam. We play by the rules,' and Adam says, 'You mean 4-1.8? Come on, Irving. This is bullshit,' and Sliman replies, 'Your issue, not mine.'"

"4-1.8?" Benny said. "What is that rule?"

"It took me half the morning to figure it out," I said. "I thought it might be a rule of Missouri civil procedure, but there isn't one numbered one-point-eight. I checked the real estate statutes, the rules governing trusts, the rules governing every Missouri administrative body I could think of that might regulate real estate transactions or apartment complexes or trusts."

"Nothing?" Jacki said.

"Nothing. But then I thought back to Danelle Knight's deposition testimony, the part were she blurted out that Adam Fox was sleeping with his client."

"And?" Benny said.

I smiled. "And I went to the Missouri Supreme Court Rules. Guess what? There is a Rule 4-1.8."

"Huh?" Benny said.

"Rule 4 contains the Rules of Professional Conduct—the ones governing attorneys. It starts at Rule 4-1.0 and goes to Rule 4-9.1."

"Okay."

"Rule 4-1.8 governs conflicts of interest for attorneys. Specifically, it governs prohibited transactions." I looked down at my notes. "There are ten subparts—subparts (a) through (k). Each one sets forth a different type of prohibited transaction."

"Such as?" Jacki asked.

I looked at my notes. "Okay. Subpart (c) says that a lawyer shall not solicit any substantial gift from a client unless the lawyer is related to the client."

I looked at Jacki, and then at Benny, and then back at my notes. "Ready? Here is how subpart (j) reads: A lawyer shall not have sexual relations with a client unless a consensual sexual relationship existed between them when the client-lawyer relationship commenced."

Jacki frowned. "Okay. And?"

I pointed to the page from the transcript of that phone call. "Look at what Sliman says to Fox. He's very careful. 'My draft solves the issue,' he says. 'I checked.' Adam Fox asks him what he checked and Sliman says 'Come on, Adam. We play by the rules,' Then Adam says, 'You mean 4-1.8? Come on, Irving. This is bullshit,' and Sliman replies, 'Your issue, not mine.' I'm sure

Sliman had raised that issue and that rule in their negotiations. But he never says it in that conversation."

I leaned back in my chair. "There."

"Holy shit," Benny said.

Jacki shook her head. "That's extortion."

"Almost," I said. "But only almost. Sliman never mentions the rule and doesn't confirm Adam's citation to the rule. He just tells Adam he'd better get the deal done as is."

"Or else," Benny said.

"But he never says 'or else.'"

Jackie nodded. "He didn't need to."

I nodded. "Adam Fox knew exactly what Sliman meant: either get your client to sign off on this deal or I'm reporting you the Chief Disciplinary Counsel, and if that happens, young man, you just might lose your law license."

"Man, oh man." Benny shook his head. "Adam Fox fucked his client every way possible."

Jacki turned to me. "So what's this mean for your case?"

"I'm not sure. I'm still trying to sort this out."

"When did Fox die?" Benny asked.

"Several months later."

"How?" Benny asked.

I reached into my briefcase, pulled out a printout of a newspaper article, and handed it to Benny. "Here."

He started reading it. "Jeez."

"What's it say?" Jacki asked.

"Poor bastard fell."

"Fell?" Jacki said. "Where?"

"Castlewood State Park. According to this, he was on some hiking trail along the bluffs overlooking the Meramec River. Slipped, fell over the edge, landed headfirst on the rocks below. Dead by the time the ambulance arrived."

"Was he on his own?" Jacki asked.

Benny kept reading. He shook his head. "No, he was on some sort of law firm outing. A team-building exercise, according to Norma Cross."

"She was there?"

"Apparently."

"What's a team-building exercise?" Jacki asked.

"Not clear from this," Benny said. "Seems she takes lawyers from her firm on different types of physical challenges—biking, kayaking, hiking, swimming. Builds camaraderie, she claims."

"Was Adam married?" Jacki asked.

Benny scanned the article and shrugged. "Doesn't say."

"He wasn't," I said. "I found his obituary. Survived by his mother and an older sister."

"Fell off a cliff," Jacki said.

"That sucks," Benny said.

Jacki turned to me. "What's the next move?"

"Irving Sliman,"

"Huh?"

"I'm meeting him tomorrow afternoon."

"No shit," Benny said. "Where?"

"At his country club. For drinks."

"Sliman?" Benny said. "Why him?"

"See if he'll tell me about his meeting with Norma Cross."

"Which meeting?" Benny asked.

Jacki said, "The one mentioned in the file. After the divorce was final."

"I haven't seen that one. What is it?"

"Three months after entry of the final judgment," I said, "Irving Sliman has his secretary send Norma Cross an e-mail asking her to meet him at the St. Louis Club."

"Regarding the divorce?" Benny asked.

"Maybe. At least that's what Norma thought. She sends back an e-mail suggesting that Sliman must have meant to send it to Adam Fox instead of her, but Irving's secretary responded that no, he wanted to meet with her, and only her."

Jacki snorted. "That was then. Don't think Norma would agree to such a meeting these days."

I looked a Jacki. "Really? Why?"

"You told me that Irving is protective of his son, Marc, right?"

"Definitely."

"And Norma would know that."

"Probably."

"A few months ago," Jacki said, "I was in Judge Warren's court on motion call. Norma Cross and Marc Sliman were on a case that got called up before mine. On opposite sides."

"A divorce?" Benny asked.

"Yep. And it was nasty."

"How so?" I asked.

"Norma had filed a motion to disqualify Marc as the husband's attorney."

"On what ground?" I asked.

"Pretty lame, I thought. Apparently, he'd represented the wife's brother in a worker's comp claim. Norma made it sound like it was some sleazy undercover operation to get confidential information about her client. Marc tried to defend himself, but it was painful to watch. He was clearly upset, and he's just not that articulate. He claimed that the worker's comp case had been resolved before the divorce case was even filed, that he didn't know who his client's sister was at the time, and that they never talked about her or her marital problems. He was rattled, though, and pretty hard to follow." She shook her head. "Marc Sliman is definitely not Irving Sliman."

"What did the judge do?" Benny asked.

"He granted Norma's motion. Disqualified Marc from the case. Poor guy was practically in tears walking out of the courtroom."

"Interesting," I said. "It tells me that Irving Sliman has his own agenda for our meeting."

"How so?" Benny asked.

"I didn't think he'd agree to meet me again."

"Why not?" Jacki asked.

"I assume he knows exactly which of his documents I've been allowed to review, which means he knows that I've seen the transcript of his final call with Adam Fox and that I've seen the last e-mail exchange with Norma Cross, all of which means he can assume I want to ask him about that final call and that meeting with Norma."

I leaned back in my chair, looked at Benny, and then at Jacki. "But he's still willing to meet with me."

"Doesn't mean he's willing to tell you anything," Jacki said.

"True." I shrugged. "But it also doesn't mean he isn't."

Chapter Twenty-two

Philip, the elderly maître d', once again greeted me at the entrance to the dining room at Golden Bough Country Club, although this time he greeted me by name.

"Ah, Miss Gold," he said, with a smile and a slight bow. "So good to see you again, young lady. Please follow me."

He led me down a wide carpeted hallway off the dining room to a door with a brass plaque that read Pere Marquette Room. He knocked twice.

"Yes?" said the familiar raspy voice from inside.

Philip opened the door and leaned in. "Your guest has arrived, sir."

"Show her in."

The maître d' turned to me as he stepped back from the door and gestured with his other hand. "Please, Miss Gold."

As I entered the room, Sliman lifted his empty whiskey glass toward the maître d' and rattled the ice.

Philip nodded. "I will tell Harold. Miss Gold, what can we get you to drink?"

I checked my wristwatch. Twenty to five. Close enough. "I'll take a glass of red wine."

"Pinot noir?"

"That's fine. Thanks."

As I took a seat across the table from my host, I heard the door close behind me. Judging from Sliman's outfit—navy sports jacket, white dress shirt with the top button unbuttoned, gray slacks—this was not a golf afternoon. His black horn-rimmed sunglasses rested atop his bald head.

We exchanged the obligatory pleasantries and small talk, though I was a bit surprised by just how much Irving Sliman knew about my private life. He asked about my mother, my sister and brother-in-law, my two stepdaughters, and my son—and all by name. It was at once charming and unsettling. And also, as I recalled, an essential element of the Sliman modus operandi. Whether cross-examining a witness, conferring with a government official, negotiating a deal, or meeting a new client, Irving Sliman came armed to the event with a deep knowledge of his counterpart's personal details.

The waiter arrived with our drinks, and when he left I shifted the conversation to my agenda—or at least what I assumed was my agenda.

"I reviewed documents from your law firm's file on the Knight divorce."

Sliman nodded. "So I understand."

"I assume you know which documents I was allowed to review."

"I would hope that my former firm complied with the court's order."

"From one of those documents—the transcript of a telephone conversation between you and Mr. Fox near the end of the case— it appears that Mr. Fox was aware that you were aware that Mr. Fox was in a sexual relationship with his client, Marsha Knight."

"So it would appear," he said, his voice neutral.

"I saw no document in that file to indicate that you'd hired a private investigator to do any surveillance of Mrs. Knight."

"There is no such document. There was no such investigation."

"Which means that either you or your client figured out that Mrs. Knight was sleeping with her lawyer."

He took a sip of his whiskey. "That seems a reasonable inference."

"And based on our last conversation, Irving, in which you invoked the attorney-client privilege on the subject, I assume it was your client who discovered the affair, not you."

He smiled. "Perhaps, Rachel, you should change your last name to Marple."

"I prefer Gold."

"Don't we all."

I paused to take a sip of wine.

"Jerry and Marsha Knight were separated at the time the divorce papers were filed," I said. "Jerry was living in his apartment. That means he didn't have access to Marsha's computer or cell phone, which means that he didn't find out about her sexual relationship with Mr. Fox by peeking at her texts or e-mails. And you've confirmed that he couldn't have found out through a private investigator, since none was hired. So that means he found out by accident. Pure luck. Right?"

Sliman took a sip of his whiskey and set the glass down. He stared at the glass for a moment and then raised his eyes, slightly amused. "Why should I answer that?"

"Why not? Your client is dead. He won't care."

"He may be dead, but his attorney-client privilege lives on."

"True. You mentioned the privilege last time, too. But he waived that privilege long ago."

"How so?"

"Your client discovered the affair. But whatever he told you about that affair you apparently passed along to Marsha Knight's lawyer, namely, Adam Fox. Thus whatever privilege might have existed prior to that was waived by your disclosure to her lawyer."

"Perhaps." He gazed at his whiskey glass a moment and then stared at me. "But back to my question: why should I tell you?"

On the drive to the country club I had considered possible responses to that very question. One option was to explain that I could subpoena him for a deposition and force him to answer my question—and if he refused, I could seek a court order requiring him to answer it. But I knew enough to know that such a threat was not a viable option with this man. To paraphrase that old Jim Croce song, you don't tug on Superman's cape, you don't spit into the wind, you don't pull the mask off that old Lone Ranger, and you don't mess around with Irving Sliman.

"Because," I said, "the only other person with any interest to protect would be your late client's widow, Danielle. Given that there is no attorney-client privilege regarding Mr. Knight's communication with you, the only reason to protect her would be out of some sense of loyalty."

I paused to take a sip of wine. "I was taught that loyalty is a two-way street. Danielle certainly hasn't been loyal to you, or to your law firm, or to your son. I'm not asking you to take sides or be anyone's advocate, Irving. I'm only asking you to tell me the truth."

He chuckled. "Not bad, young lady. A clever pitch. It might even persuade someone other than me. But that's no matter, since I don't need persuading. You're right about the waiver of the privilege. I disclosed Jerry's discovery of his wife's infidelity with his express consent. He understood that such a disclosure to opposing counsel might, well, shall we say, provide him some bargaining leverage. Pure speculation, of course. But it was my client's decision, not mine."

I smiled. "So tell me. How did he find out?"

"The great Branch Rickey once said that luck is the residue of design. Not so here. The discovery was pure coincidence. My client had spent the prior weekend with his daughter, Katie, and dropped her off Sunday night after dinner. When he got back to his apartment, he discovered that she'd left her history textbook there. Ever the dutiful father, on his way to the office early the following morning he drove by the house to drop it off. But as he pulled up he saw an unfamiliar car in the driveway. Curious, he jotted down the license plate and then backed up his car to the end of the block to wait. The house was only three doors down, so he had a clear view of the front door and the driveway. At roughly seven-twenty a.m., about ten minutes before his daughter's alarm would go off, the front door opened. Who should step out onto the porch? Adam Fox, accompanied by Marsha Knight in a flimsy negligee. They kissed. Passionately, according to Jerry. Adam got into his car, pulled out of the driveway, and drove down the block to the stop sign, where Jerry lightly tapped the

horn once, Adam looked over, eyes wide, and quickly drove off.
Jerry waited a few minutes, drove over to the school, dropped
Katie's textbook off at the front office, and then came directly
to my office." He took another sip of whiskey and leaned back
in his chair. "All in all, a most productive morning for Jerry."

"Did Adam tell Marsha what happened?"

"I have no idea. Probably not."

"Did you ever ask him?"

"Never. I never even mentioned the incident to him."

"Other than that reference to his violation of that ethics rule."

"Actually, his reference, not mine. An oblique and ambiguous
reference at best, I think you would agree."

"That was the first time?"

"That was the *only* time, at least on the record. And as you
know, Mr. Fox merely stated a number. He didn't identify the
name of that rule or where it could be found. You have apparently located one such rule with that particular number within
the Missouri Code of Professional Responsibility. I commend
your ingenuity, Rachel. Of course, there are many subparts to
that rule, assuming that is the one that Mr. Fox was referring to."

I took of sip of wine and gazed at him. "Tell me, Irving. Why
did you agree to meet me today?"

"Why not? I am retired. Why should an old man in his dotage
spurn an opportunity to meet with an intelligent and beautiful
young woman?"

I smiled. "That's your story and you're sticking with it, eh?"

He chuckled. "I am, indeed."

"So the case settles," I said. "Final judgment is entered, and
then three months later, according to the final document in that
file, you meet with Norma Cross."

"I did."

"At your request."

"Correct."

"Why?"

He frowned. "It's complicated."

"Try me."

"Within the legal community I had a certain reputation, a persona, you might say, that was no doubt effective in many of my dealings with other attorneys and their clients but was, I concede, somewhat of a caricature. Indeed, the *Riverfront Times* once labeled me the Godfather of the St. Louis Bar. As you might imagine, during the months after that article appeared, more than one attorney and even a few judges called me Don Corleone or Tony Soprano. It was amusing, I suppose, but also a bit irritating. I was proud to be an attorney, Rachel, and I tried to adhere to the Code of Professional Responsibility. During my forty-five-year career, I never had an ethics charge filed against me. Never. And while I had several opportunities over the years, many quite tempting, I never had sex with a client. Never. And thus Mr. Fox's malfeasance bothered me. I brooded over it for a couple months, and once or twice even considered filing my own ethics complaint, but eventually decided that instead I would simply disclose his malfeasance to his boss. There is, I acknowledge, more than a little irony in disclosing an employee's ethical violation to someone as ethically challenged and morally compromised as Norma Cross, but I decided to do it anyway. Let her deal with it."

"So you told her at that meeting at the St. Louis Club."

"I did."

"How did she respond?"

"She was angry. But then again, she is always angry." Irving Sliman took a final sip of his whiskey, set the glass down, and gazed at me for a long moment. "She was also dismayed."

"Okay."

"Unusually dismayed," he said.

"How so?"

He pursed his lips and rubbed his chin. "Let's just say I detected a personal element to her dismay. Very personal."

I frowned. "What do you mean?"

He smiled. "Exactly what I just said. And that is all I shall say on that subject."

He checked his watch, raised his eyebrows, and got to his feet. "Unfortunately, Rachel, I have another engagement starting down the hall in just five minutes."

I stood. "Thank you, Irving."

He smiled as he lowered his sunglasses to his eyes. "I have thoroughly enjoyed our little tête-à-tête. I wish you good luck in your matter."

Chapter Twenty-three

Benny finished his beer, set down the bottle, looked at Jacki, and then at me. "Really? You think Adam was shtupping Norma, too?"

I shrugged. "What else could Irving have meant?"

"What were his words again?" Jacki asked.

"He said that he detected a personal element to her dismay. A *very personal* element."

Jacki frowned. "Maybe. But maybe instead she was Adam's mentor at the firm. If so, maybe she took his ethical violation personally."

Benny snorted. "Norma Cross? Come on, Jacki. From what I understand, that fucking she-devil built her career on ethical violations."

"Maybe," Jacki said, "but you'd be surprised how many sleazeballs view themselves as pillars of morality." She turned to me. "Such as Slimeball."

The three of us were having a late dinner at my house. I'd invited Jacki and Benny to come by at seven-thirty so that I'd have enough time to put Sam to bed. I'd made a big salad, and Sam and I baked an apple galette for dessert. I gave him a slice as a bedtime snack. Jacki brought two deep-dish pizzas from Pi. Benny was supposed to bring the beer, which he did: one six-pack of Schlafly Pale Ale and one six-pack of Schlafly Oatmeal Stout. But Benny being Benny, he also stopped by Pappy's Smokehouse and picked up what he described as a little *farshpayz* (Yiddish for appetizer), namely, a half-dozen spicy sausages, three of which he'd already consumed along with half of one of the pizzas. The man has capacity.

Jacki turned to me. "So what do you think?"

I shook my head. "Crazy as it sounds, I think Adam Fox may have been Norma's boyfriend."

"As in 'serious' boyfriend?" Benny asked.

"I think so."

"So when Slimeball tells her about Adam," Jacki said, "she's dismayed for a genuinely personal reason."

I nodded. "That's how I read it."

Benny said, "You think Sliman knew that Fox was her boyfriend?"

I shrugged. "Hard to say. The way he described his meeting with her, he seemed surprised by her reaction."

"Man, oh man." Benny leaned back in his chair and chuckled. "From what I've heard about Norma Cross, that is one woman you do not want cheat on."

Jacki turned to me. "Which raises another question…why would Slimeball tell you about that meeting?"

"Good question," I said.

"Out of spite?" she said. "Because of what she did to his son in that court case?"

"Maybe. He's protective of his son."

"Remind me," Benny said. "When did Fox die?"

"About four weeks after that meeting," Jacki said.

As I put water on for tea, I mulled over the possible implications of that time line. I took out the teacups and put a slice of the galette on each dessert plate while Benny and Jacki rinsed the dishes and put them in the dishwasher.

Benny virtually inhaled his first slice of the galette.

"Whoa, girlfriend!" He gave me a thumbs-up. "Pie is awesome."

I smiled. "Thanks."

"How's that other case?" Jacki asked, gesturing toward Benny. "The one Mr. Wonderful here is going to help you try next week."

"Cyndi and I are meeting at that DNA company tomorrow afternoon."

"They have the results?" Benny asked.

"Apparently."

"And?"

I shrugged. "We'll find out tomorrow."

"Does Bert Mulligan's son know about this DNA outfit?" Jacki asked.

"No. We've kept it confidential. Just in case."

"Just in case the results suck," Benny said.

I nodded. "Just in case."

"Keep your fingers crossed," Jacki said.

I held up both hands, fingers crossed.

Chapter Twenty-four

Mouse Aloni.

What goes around comes around. In more ways than one. Here I was, nearly ten years later, a decade after the Stoddard Anderson affair, seated once again across the desk from Detective Mario "Mouse" Aloni.

The last time we sat across from one another, Aloni was a detective with the Bridgeton Police Department and I was representing the widow of the managing partner of the St. Louis office of Abbott & Windsor. My client's husband had apparently committed suicide in a motel room in Bridgeton. What began as a seemingly straightforward battle over life insurance proceeds escalated into a deadly international conspiracy involving a legendary archaeological treasure.

This time, Aloni was a homicide detective with the St. Louis County Police Department, and I was representing Jerry Knight's first wife, Marsha, whose divorce attorney had fallen to his death during a hike along the bluffs overlooking the Meramec River in Castlewood State Park. And, fortunately for me, Aloni was also on good terms with Bertie Tomaso, a homicide detective with the Metropolitan Police Department of the City of St. Louis and a dear friend of mine. Bertie had made the call to arrange this meeting.

Mouse.

The nickname had baffled me ten years ago. Stretch would have made more sense, since he was as tall as an NBA forward. Or Slim, since he was skinny. Or Curly or Fuzzy, one of those antonym nicknames for bald men. But Mouse? Perched behind his cheap metal desk, hunched forward as he studied the file, long face, hooked nose, dark brown eyes beneath bushy projecting eyebrows, he looked more like a winged predator, the type that swoops down and carries off a mouse in its talons.

The nickname, I had learned back then, originated in his preference for cheese sandwiches, which he packed in a brown paper bag when he brought lunch from home and which he ordered, grilled, when he had lunch in a restaurant. Cheese every day, and always American.

Mouse looked up at me with a frown. "This case has been closed for years, ma'am. It was ruled an accident." He shook his head. "They happen. This isn't the first death at Castlewood, ma'am. And this gentleman was not the first one to fall to his death from those bluffs."

"Were there any witnesses?"

He leafed slowly through the file again and then shook his head. "None at the time of the fall." He looked up. "Hardly surprising. The accident occurred on a Monday morning. That is a slow day at the park. Especially in the morning."

"You said none at the time of the fall. What about before or after the fall?"

"Just his hiking companion."

"Norma Cross?"

He looked up, bushy eyebrows raised. "Yes, that's right. She was the person that made the 911 call."

"But she didn't see him fall?"

He looked down at the file, read something, and looked up. "No. She was ahead of him on the trail. She heard some noise and turned. The decedent was not behind her. She didn't see him. She worked her way back along that trail, calling his name, peering over the edge of the bluffs."

He glanced down at the file for a moment and then back up. "She saw his body sprawled out on the rocks below. She didn't have cell phone reception there, so she hurried back down the trail until she had reception, and that's when she called 911.

She was quite upset." He glanced down at the file again. "The decedent was an employee of her law firm. A lawyer, in fact."

"Was there an autopsy?"

He leafed through the file. "Yes, there was."

He lifted a stapled set of papers and frowned as he read them. "Let's see."

He turned the page, read some, and looked up. "He was not intoxicated. His blood alcohol level was less than point-zero-one." He looked up at me and shook his head. "Accidents happen, ma'am."

"Can I have a copy of the autopsy report?"

Mouse frowned. "Why?"

"I'm trying to tie up some loose ends for a client. The autopsy report may help me do that."

"The case is closed, ma'am."

"Good. Then there shouldn't be a problem."

Mouse stared at me for a moment and then looked down. "I don't know about that."

"I do, Detective. You said yourself the case is closed. Under the sunshine laws, once it's closed, those records become public records. There is no reason to make me jump through any hoops. Just make a photocopy and I'm gone."

He rubbed his chin.

"Well?" I said.

"I'll have to ask my captain. It's his call. Just like last time."

"What do you mean—just like last time?"

"On releasing a copy."

"Of that autopsy report?"

"I believe so."

"So someone else has asked for a copy?"

He stood, the folder in his hands. "I believe so, yes."

"Who?"

He pursed his lips and tilted his head, as if thinking it over. "I'm not sure. It was a few years ago. Anyway, the captain is the one who needs to approve the release of a copy to you."

I sighed. "Then do it, Detective. Now. Please."

Chapter Twenty-five

Thursday afternoon.

Cyndi and I were seated in a small conference room at the offices of AssureDNA Company. As we waited, I went over the logistics of the hearing set for next Monday.

"Judge Bauer is a no-nonsense judge," I told her. "The hearing is scheduled for eleven a.m., and that means eleven a.m. sharp. If you're late, he starts without you. When you are—"

There was a rap on the door, and then a tall bearded man in his forties in a white lab coated entered carrying a manila folder.

"I am so sorry for the delay," he said. "I hope you have not been waiting long. I'm Dr. Bryant. Phil Bryant."

We introduced ourselves and shook hands. Bryant took a seat at the head of the table and set the manila folder down in front of him. After a few minutes of polite chitchat, he opened the folder and put on his reading glasses.

"We received the DNA results this morning." He turned to Cyndi. "As I explained to Ms. Gold at the outset, Mrs. Mulligan, the analysis is more challenging than your standard paternity test, which is where we compare the DNA of the child with that of his or her putative father. The dilution in that situation is just fifty percent, since half of the child's DNA comes from the child's biological father. In your typical paternity case, the test results lead to one of two conclusions: either a greater than nine-nine percent certainty of paternity or a one hundred percent certainty of non-paternity. Unfortunately, the identification challenge increases geometrically the farther away the DNA donor is from the potential father. Here we are comparing the child's DNA to the DNA of the female daughter of a female sibling of the potential father."

"And?" I said.

Bryant studied two of the pages as he scratched his beard. He looked up at me, his lips pursed in thought.

"I have never testified as an expert in court," he said.

"You may not need to here."

"Even so, I want to choose my words carefully." He paused. "Do these test results prove that Mr. Mulligan is the child's father? No, they do not. Do these test results prove that Mr. Mulligan is not the father? No, they do not. Do the test results provide us with any probabilities regarding Mr. Mulligan and the child? Yes, they do. The test results provide at least a fifty percent probability of a familial connection between Mr. Mulligan and the child. Stated differently, it is slightly more likely than not that he is related to the child."

I stared at him, replaying his words in my head, my mind racing.

"More likely than not," I repeated.

He nodded. "That is my opinion."

After a moment, I stood. "Thank you, Doctor. This has been extremely helpful. I will let you know tomorrow whether we will need you to testify on Monday."

Out in the parking lot I pulled Cyndi close. "I have an idea."

"Oh?" She said it without enthusiasm. "I was hoping we'd get something a heck of lot more conclusive."

"We might be able to get there on our own."

"How?"

"You told me that Bert gave you the access code for his vials of sperm, right?"

"He did, but it's not something you could memorize. It was like fifteen random numbers and letters."

"So how did he actually give you the number?"

"On a piece of paper."

"Why on a piece of paper?"

"So I could give it to the doctor."

I smiled. "Exactly."

She gave me a puzzled look. "So?"

"Cyndi, your doctor will still have that number. It should be in his records for you."

She frowned. "Okay."

"I want you to talk to him today. As soon as you get home. Tell him it's important. Tell him you need that number. Tell him I'm your lawyer. Tell him I want to talk to him."

"Really?"

"Yes, really."

"Well, okay."

"It's important, Cyndi. Call me as soon as you talk to him."

"Okay."

I smiled. "Hang in there."

"I'm trying, Rachel." Her eyes watered. "It's not easy."

"I know." I gave her a hug. "But it's almost over."

Chapter Twenty-six

Professor of Pathology.

It's a grim title, made all the more incongruous by its holder, my elementary school classmate Izzy Feigelman. Little, chubby, brilliant, and sweet back then, and little, chubby, brilliant, and sweet today. But now bald, having finally given up on the comb-over.

We'd become pals in fourth grade, remained friends in high school despite moving in very different circles by then. We were even lab partners in our biology class where, ironically, I had to dissect the frog because the future pathologist nearly fainted at the sight of blood. Izzy and I still get together for lunch once or twice a year. He married Naomi Burstein, who was a year behind us in high school, and they have three kids, ranging in age from six down to six months.

Izzy is now Dr. Isadore Mendel Feigelman, M.D., Professor of Pathology, Washington University School of Medicine. I knew of no one better to read the Adam Fox autopsy report.

We met that afternoon at Izzy's office at Barnes Jewish Hospital, which was a three-block walk from my law office in the Central West End. I'd stopped at the Starbucks on the way over to pick up Izzy's favorite, a caramel macchiato. He was sipping it as he studied the several pages of the autopsy report.

He nodded approvingly. "Very thorough."

"He has an older sister," I said. "According to the detective, she insisted on a full autopsy."

He scribbled a note on his legal pad, turned the page, took another sip of his drink, scribbled something else on his pad.

Another page, another sip, another scribble.

My cell phone buzzed. A text message from a client. I typed a response, pressed Send, and flipped through my e-mails as Izzy continued his methodical way through the report.

"Well, well." he said.

I looked up. "What?"

"This blood test report."

"What about it?"

"It's from a sample taken from the decedent's heart."

"His heart? Is that typical?"

"Not usually, but for a thorough autopsy, yes."

"And?"

"There is an elevated level of GHB."

"What's GHB?"

"Gamma hydroxybutyric acid."

"Okay. And what is gamma-hy-whatever?"

"It's actually a naturally occurring substance found in the human central nervous system. Not just humans, either. GHB exists in small amounts in almost all animals. Indeed, you can even find GHB in citrus fruits and wine."

"You said the blood sample showed an elevated level."

"It did."

"What does that mean?"

"Here's where it gets somewhat more complex, Rachel. There are natural elevated levels and artificially elevated levels."

"Explain."

"GHB is present in the blood and the urine of the general population as an endogenous compound, and that endogenous level actually increases postmortem."

"In English, Izzy, please."

He smiled and shrugged. "Sorry. Okay, so GHB is a naturally occurring compound. If we took a blood sample from someone and did a state-of-the-art blood test, we'd detect the presence of GHB. But here's where it gets tricky. If we took another blood sample from that same person but after he'd been dead for several hours, the GHB level would be higher than when he was alive."

"Okay. And why does this matter?"

"Because—" and here he paused to lean forward, eyebrows raised, face flushed with what I could only describe as geek excitement "—because a toxicologist needs to be able to discriminate between endogenous levels and a level resulting from exogenous exposure. Due to the wide distribution of endogenous concentrations of GHB in postmortem toxicology, the implementation of a cut-off concentration must be done cautiously."

"Come on, Izzy. I was an English major. Help me out here."

"Rachel, haven't you heard of GHB?"

I frowned "I don't think so."

"It's a drug. A controlled substance. There are legitimate medical uses for it. It's been used as a general anesthetic, although not much anymore. It's still used to treat insomnia, clinical depression, and narcolepsy. But it has illegal uses, too."

"Really? Such as…"

"It goes by many nicknames on the street. Bedtime Scoop. Cherry Meth. Easy Lay. Georgia Home Boy. In lower doses, it's a recreational drug. But in higher doses—" he paused and leaned back in his chair, shaking his head sadly "—it's been used as a date-rape drug."

"What does it do?"

"Pretty much what you'd expect. It will induce dizziness, drowsiness, visual disturbances, agitation, amnesia. Often, unconsciousness, and sometime death."

"How is it taken?"

"When used recreationally or as a date-rape drug, it comes in the form of a white crystalline powder. It's odorless and, when dissolved in a liquid, colorless. The most common version tastes salty, but there are versions that are less salty. And depending upon the liquid, that flavor can be masked."

I absorbed that information, struggling to make sense of it.

"And there," I said, gesturing toward the autopsy report. "The GHB level?"

"That is a level of concentration most likely the result of exogenous exposure."

"In other words, Izzy, he took GHB that morning?"

"In my opinion, yes."

I leaned back in the chair. After a moment, I said, "Izzy."

"Yes?"

I gestured toward the autopsy paperwork. "If you could figure all of that out from the autopsy report, someone else in your field—someone good—could do it, too, right?"

"If they were suspicious and if they were up to speed on the latest research in that area, sure. But that's not always the case with a county medical examiner, if that's what you're thinking."

"No." I frowned. "Someone else asked for a copy of that autopsy report."

"When?"

"Apparently, a few years ago."

"Who?"

"I don't know. The police wouldn't tell me."

"His sister? You said she was the one who insisted on the full autopsy."

"No. The records show that she received her own copy at the time it was created. This other copy—that was later. There's no record of it." I shook my head. "I keep wondering who. And why?"

Chapter Twenty-seven

I spent the rest of that afternoon drafting court papers for Marsha Knight's case, and the following morning I filed my motion to add the Cross Law Firm as a third-party defendant in Danielle Knight's lawsuit against Marsha. The third-party petition was a straightforward malpractice claim. It alleged that if the court should void the divorce-case bequest to Marsha because of the Rule Against Perpetuities, then her loss was solely the result of her attorney's malpractice, namely, his authorization of a property settlement for his client that violated the Rule Against Perpetuities.

I filed the court papers at ten a.m., and arranged for the process server to deliver them to Danielle Knight's attorney and to Norma Cross by noon. I met Benny for lunch at Pho Grand to go over our courtroom strategy for Cyndi Mulligan's "bloodline" case, which was set for trial the following Monday. By the time I returned to the office that afternoon, my office phone voicemail inbox included three increasingly threatening voicemail messages from Norma Cross.

The first was relatively civil, at least by Norma Cross standards: "This is Norma Cross. I just received a copy of your court papers in the Knight case. I am, to put it mildly, shocked. Shocked. Call me immediately."

The second message, received thirty-one minutes later, was a bit more heated: "This is my second call to you. I expect the professional courtesy of a prompt response. Call me to discuss your fucking ridiculous third-party claim against my law firm. How dare you? Call me. Now! I am waiting."

And she had waited, according to my voicemail system, for twenty-two minutes before calling a third time: "This is Norma. For the third goddamned time, bitch! Why don't you suck it up, little girl, crawl out from under your desk, and call me? If I haven't heard back from you in the next fifteen minutes, you'll get my response by messenger delivery this afternoon."

And I did.

At four-twenty that afternoon a delivery service dropped off a copy of Norma's Motion to Strike Third-Party Petition and for Sanctions, along with a notice setting the matter for an emergency hearing the following morning at ten a.m.

And at 10:06 the following morning, Judge Harry Ballsack's courtroom clerk called out, "Knight versus Knight. Motion of the Cross Law Firm to Strike Third-Party Petition and for Sanctions."

And once again, the three of us—me in the middle, Tom Sterling to my left, Norma Cross to my right—approached the podium. This time, however, the Honorable Harry Ballsack scowled down at Norma Cross.

"An emergency? Really? Where's the fire?"

"Right in this courtroom, Your Honor. This woman—"

"Show some respect, Counsel. You are in a courtroom, not a barroom."

Norma frowned. "Pardon?"

"This woman?!" the judge said, his voice rising. "She is a licensed attorney. You either refer to her as 'counsel' or you can refer yourself right out of here. Now take a deep breath and start over. As the Court previously asked you, what is the emergency?"

"This attorney—"

"You mean 'counsel for defendant,' correct?"

"Yes."

Judge Ballsack leaned over the bench, his face red. "Then! Say! It!"

I was beginning to enjoy this hearing.

Norma stepped back from the podium, pursed her lips together, and then stepped forward. "Counsel for defendant has filed a motion to add my law firm as a third-party defendant."

"I see that, Miss Cross. The motion is in the court file. According to my clerk, the matter is set for hearing next Friday. Miss Gold gave proper notice under the rules of civil procedure. Again, Ms. Cross, what is the emergency today?"

"Her motion is outrageous."

"So you say. I will now ask for the fourth and last time: what is the emergency today?"

"Her motion needs to be denied immediately. It needs to be expunged from the public records of this court. Her accusations—"

"Her, Ms. Cross? Who, pray tell, is this 'her'?"

She turned to me with a sneer. "This…woman. Counsel for defendant."

"And of what has counsel for defendant accused your firm?"

"Malpractice. She has libeled and she has defamed my law firm and, even worse, she has besmirched the reputation and the honor of a dead man. I will not stand for it."

"And this is what you contend justifies an emergency hearing?"

"Absolutely. So long as that defamatory third-party complaint remains in the court file, my law firm and our esteemed dead associate suffer ongoing irreparable harm."

The judge turned to Tom Sterling. "Your position, Counsel?"

"We're neutral, Your Honor. Like the last time, our dog isn't in this fight. We're just passive onlookers."

The judge snorted. "More like rubberneckers, if you ask me."

Sterling smiled and shrugged.

The judge turned to me. "And you, Counsel?"

"There is no emergency, Your Honor. This matter is set for a hearing next Friday. If Ms. Cross has an issue, she can raise it then. But, frankly, there is no issue. As we set forth in our court papers, Your Honor, the sole ground plaintiff asserts for voiding the property settlement is the Rule Against Perpetuities. While we disagree with that position, in the unlikely event that this

Court were to rule in plaintiff's favor, our position is that such a ruling would necessarily lead to a finding of malpractice by the law firm that represented my client in that divorce. That law firm is the Cross Law Firm. Ms. Cross has twice made reference to the document being in the public files of the courthouse. If that is her concern, there's an easy solution. We don't object to having our petition filed under seal. That should resolve Counsel's problem."

"That," Norma Cross, "would hardly resolve—"

The judge banged his gavel. "Excellent point, Ms. Gold!

He paused to glare at Norma.

"This Court has heard enough. By the powers invested in me by the State of Missouri, I hereby deny the emergency motion of the Cross Law Firm. And while we're at it, I will save all of you a trip down here next Friday." He gave me a smile. "This Court grants your motion for leave to file that third-party petition and orders that said petition be filed under seal. Draft me an order, Ms. Gold."

He leaned forward and glared down at Norma. "Next case!"

As I was over at the side table drafting the order denying Norma's motion and granting mine, she stepped close, leaned over, and hissed, "You will regret this day, little girl. That's my guarantee."

I ignored her and kept writing.

Chapter Twenty-eight

Shannon McCarthy shrugged. "It just didn't make sense to me."

"What part?" I asked.

"The way he died. Falling off that cliff or bluff or whatever it's called."

"How so?"

"Adam was a mountain climber."

"He wasn't the first person to fall and die at Castlewood Park."

"Look, Miss Gold, I don't know much about mountain climbing, but my brother was a serious one. He climbed Mount Ranier out in Washington after law school, and then a year before he died he climbed Half Dome in Yosemite. I've seen his pictures. Those are big-time climbs—and dangerous ones, too. Cliffs, glaciers, you name it. But Castlewood? On a sunny day? I've walked along that same gravel path. It was filled with kids and families."

Shannon McCarthy and I were seated at a small table near the back of the St. Louis Bread Company in South City. Her choice. Near her house. It was mid-morning. We both had cups of coffee and were splitting a bear claw.

I had called Shannon yesterday afternoon to see if she had an hour to spare to meet with me. I kept it vague, saying that I had a case that involved a matter her younger brother had worked on. She'd agreed, somewhat reluctantly. From what I had been able to determine online, Shannon was in her late thirties, married, mother of two, and apparently not presently employed outside the home.

"I spoke with Detective Aloni," I said.

"Okay."

Shannon was a large blonde—in both height and weight—with black glasses and thick, wavy, shoulder-length hair. There was a frazzled, agitated aura about her, accented by the way she flipped back her hair with her hands every few minutes She was wearing baggy gray sweatpants, a St. Louis Blues tee-shirt, and white tennis shoes.

I said, "He gave me a copy of the autopsy report. He said you'd requested a full autopsy."

"I did."

"Why?"

"I just told you why." She brushed back her hair. "Because Adam's death didn't make sense."

"What did you think the autopsy would show?"

She shook her head. "Something to help me make sense of it."

"Such as?"

She shrugged. "I don't know. Like maybe he had a heart attack. Or a stroke. Or maybe he'd been drinking." She gave me a sad smile. "My brother liked to drink."

"But he wasn't drunk," I said.

"No, he wasn't." She sighed. "I don't know. I guess I hoped the autopsy would help me understand. It didn't."

"Did you talk to Norma Cross?"

"I did."

"And?"

She shook her head and then brushed her hair back with her hand. "It was a mystery to her, too. She was ahead of him on the path. She didn't hear him fall."

"Did Adam ever talk to you about Norma?"

Shannon frowned. "What do you mean?"

"Just curious. Did he ever say anything about her?"

She thought about it. "I think he liked her. I mean, she was his boss and all, but he seemed to like working with her. But she was also a tough cookie. Especially with the lawyers on the other side. But Adam liked that part." She smiled. "He said it made her sexy."

"Anything else?"

She stared at me. "What's this all about?"

"I'm trying to tie up some loose ends. Adam handled a divorce case for a woman I represent. It turns out, well, that he was more than just her lawyer."

She gave me another sad smile. "That's my little brother, God bless him. Women liked him, and he sure liked women."

"Did he mention her? Marsha Knight?"

She brushed back her hair and frowned. "Marsha Knight? I don't remember that name."

"There were others?"

"Oh, yes. Plenty of others. My husband used to say Adam had a zipper problem."

"What about his boss?"

Her eyes widened. "Norma Cross?"

I nodded.

"Jesus. Was he sleeping with her, too?"

"I don't know."

She leaned back in her chair. "What are you saying?"

I shrugged. "Just asking."

She frowned. "Norma Cross."

I took a sip of my coffee and waited.

Shannon stared down at the table. She reached for her coffee cup, started to lift it, and then set it back down. She lifted her gaze. "What does that mean? I mean, if he was, you know, banging his boss?"

On the drive to the restaurant I'd debated how to answer that very question, whether to mention Izzy Feigelman's observation about the elevated level of GBH in Adam's blood. I'd decided it was too soon and too speculative.

I said, "It may not mean anything, Shannon. How often did you see your brother?"

She thought about it. "Not that often." She brushed back

her hair. "My life is kind of crazy these days, and he was always working. We'd have him over for dinner every few weeks."

"Did you talk to him much?"

"Not that much. We'd text more than talk."

"Do you still have any of those texts?"

"Probably." She sighed. "I used to look at them a lot after he died. I'm pretty sure I still have them. Let me see."

She took a cell phone out of her purse, opened the screen, and scrolled around.

"Oh, my." She looked up, tears in her eyes, and nodded. "I still have lots of them."

I gave her a sympathetic smile, thinking of all the texts from Jonathan that I'd printed out after his funeral.

She took a bite of the bear claw and then a sip of coffee. I waited.

After a moment, she said, "I'm okay."

I handed her one of my business cards. "My cell phone is here, Shannon. If you don't mind, maybe you could send me those texts when you have some free time? I won't disclose them to anyone without your permission."

"Okay."

"Going back to that Marsha Knight case, your brother's opponent was a man named Irving Sliman. Did he ever mention Irving to you?"

She frowned and brushed back her hair. "That name sounds familiar. I don't think Adam liked him."

"Do you remember why?"

"No. Maybe it's in one of his texts."

Her cell phone dinged. She looked down, read some message, typed a response, and pressed Send.

"I'm so sorry, Miss Gold, but I'm going to have to go."

"Don't be sorry, Shannon. I really appreciate your making time to see me. And please call me Rachel."

She smiled as she stood. "Okay. Rachel."

"Take the rest of the bear claw."

She laughed. "No, thanks. Look at me." She patted her stomach. "I already have too many bear claws in there."

I stood and reached out my hand. "I'm sorry for your loss, Shannon."

"Thank you."

We shook hands.

She studied my face. "Please let me know if you find out something about Adam's death. He was my brother. My only brother."

"I will."

We hugged, and she left. I sat back down, took a sip of coffee, made a couple of notes on my legal pad, took another sip of coffee, glanced over at the bear claw, and, finally, gave in.

Chapter Twenty-nine

I watched as Jacki Brand leafed slowly through the document, which consisted of twelve pages of Adam Fox's text-message correspondence with his sister. Shannon had forwarded the entire set of texts to me, and I'd printed out two copies—one for Jacki, one for me.

Adam had died almost six years ago. Shannon's saved texts dated back nine years, and thus covered the last three years of his life. For the most part, the texts were pretty much what you'd expect to see from two adult siblings—a married sister with kids and her bachelor brother. Sometime they'd text one another several times a day. Then there'd be days, and even a week or so, of silence, followed by a burst of texts—about dinner at Shannon's house, about a birthdaya party for her son, about tickets for a Cardinals game. Adam occasionally sent his sister links to funny videos, to which she usually responded LOL!! Thanks, Bro!! Sometimes he'd break a week or two of silence with a What up, Sis? and then they'd exchange a few updates.

Jacki closed the printout and looked at me. "Okay. And?"

"Our start date is March tenth of that last year."

"What's March tenth?"

"The day Sliman told Norma about Adam's relationship with Marsha Knight."

"Ah. Got it."

"Top of page eleven. I've read through the prior ten pages

several times, looking for some reference to Marsha or to anything about his having sex with Norma."

"And?"

I shook my head. "Nada."

"When did he die?"

"April fifth. Almost a month after Irving told Norma about Adam and Marsha."

Jacki nodded. "Okay." She gestured toward the printout. "And?"

"Re-read those last two pages. See what you think."

Jacki and I had gathered in our conference room at the end of the day to review the text messages and discuss strategies for the upcoming trial in Danielle Knight's Rule-Against-Perpetuities claim against Marsha Knight.

The last text exchange before March tenth was on March third and started with Adam:

- Hey, Sis, ideas for Erin's b-day present?
- Hmm...she loves The Little Mermaid. An Ariel toy? Maybe a bath toy. Target has them.
- Great. Thanks. When's the party start on Saturday?
- 2 pm.
- See you then.
- Bye, Bro.

The next exchange was on March 14th and started with Shannon:

- Hey. u ok?
- Yeah. Why?
- Haven't heard from u.
- I'm fine.
- Busy?
- Yeah. Lot of shit going down.

- Good shit?
- With clients, yeah.
- What about the rest?
- So-so. Boss is super bitchy.
- At you?
- Yeah, probably others, too. She's been in a bad mood.
- Maybe she's on the rag. Hang in there, Bro.
- Thanks, Sis.
- Love ya.
- Back at ya.

There were a couple short exchanges the following week. On March 21st, Adam sent his sister a text telling her to check out a video on YouTube with a link to the video, which was a funny John Stewart piece on Sarah Palin from *The Daily Show*, to which Shannon replied: "OMG!! LOL!! Thanks, Bro!" The other, on March 27th, was an exchange regarding dinner that night at Shannon's house, with Adam checking on the time and seeing whether he could bring anything. The answer:

6pm. Just bring yourself. Unless you have a significant other?? (Hint, hint.)

To which Adam replied:

Sigh. My only significant other these days is a six-pack of Bud Light, which I'll bring.

And then the final exchange, on the afternoon of Sunday, April 4:

- Hubby snagged an extra ticket to the Blues game tonight! Against Blackhawks! You free?
- Damn! Early day tomorrow. Have to pass. Thank Bobby for me.

- How early??
- 7 am. "Team-building exercise."
- What's that?
- Norma's thing. Few times a year. Whatever.
- Everyone in the office?
- Sometimes, sometime not.
- Who tomorrow?
- Don't know.
- Where and what?
- Castlewood. A hike, I think.
- 7 am. Wow. Drink lots of coffee.
- She's bringing Starbucks. And donuts. Only bright side.
- Enjoy.
- Maybe.
- Love ya.
- Same. Enjoy the game, Sis.

When Jacki looked up, I said, "Well?"

"Coffee and donuts, eh?"

I nodded.

"Did she really bring them?"

"I called Izzy. He checked the autopsy report. The stomach contents were examined but not saved, probably because no one suspected any drug cause. The medical examiner described the contents as consisting of partially digested pastry or bread. So yes, she must have brought coffee and donuts."

"And put the GBH in the coffee?"

I shrugged. "Maybe."

"And we'll never prove it."

"I know."

"Not that it's actually relevant to Marsha's lawsuit."

"But very relevant to Adam's sister."

"Good Lord." Jacki shook her head. "That is a creepy crew. You've got Adam Fox, who's cheating on Norma Cross by sleeping with his own client, Marsha Knight. You've got Marsha's soon-to-be ex-husband, Jerry, who figures out that Adam is fucking Marsha and tells his lawyer. You've got his lawyer, Slimeball, who sees an opportunity to blackmail Adam into approving a property settlement that violates the Rule Against Perpetuities so that Jerry—or his widow—will be able to invalidate the deed whenever the time seems right. And then, just to twist the knife a little more, Slimeball tells Adam's boss, who's so pissed when she learns about Adam's cheating that she decides to kill him." Jackie leaned back in her chair. "Not one hero in that crew."

"But there is a client."

"True. And we're her lawyers."

"Marsha also happens to be the most innocent member of that crew. And—" I smiled. "—there just may be a way to kill all those other birds with our one stone."

"Oh, yeah?"

I shrugged. "Maybe."

"How?"

"Not to mix our metaphors, but before we pick up that litigation stone, we need to plant a seed."

"Where?"

"With Norma's lawyer."

"She has a lawyer?"

"She does now. She apparently notified her malpractice carrier. I assume the carrier retained him."

"Who's her lawyer?"

I smiled. "That's the good news."

"Oh?"

"Larry Blatz."

Jacki raised her eyebrows. "That obnoxious blowhard. He's now in the case? That's supposed to be good news?"

"I'm hoping. He's coming over tomorrow to talk with us about the case."

"His idea?"

I winked. "So he thinks."

Jacki frowned. "What's the plan?"

I leaned back in my chair. "When I was a first-year associate at Abbott & Windsor in Chicago, I worked on one case with this elderly partner named Maxwell Patrick. His nickname was Mad Max, and he'd earned it. He was as wily and unconventional as any trial lawyer I've ever known. He gave me this piece of advice: When your client's case is going nowhere, when it's stuck in some litigation logjam, look around for a hand grenade. There's always one lying around and no one else sees it. Grab it, pull the pin, toss it into the middle of the lawsuit, and in the chaos after it explodes be ready to grab any advantage you see."

Jacki was grinning. "So our hand grenade is Larry Blatz?"

"That's my hope."

"And we're going to pull the pin tomorrow?"

I smiled. "We're sure going to try."

Chapter Thirty

Larry Blatz's three most distinctive qualities were his laugh, his self-confidence, and his enormous head. His laugh was as loud and rhythmic and obnoxious as a braying donkey, complete with the squeaking gasp between each roar. His self-confidence was all the more remarkable given his mediocre legal talent. And that head of his, topped with an unruly clump of brown hair, was massive enough to give any prospective wife pause at the prospect of birthing one of his children. So massive, in fact, that last summer, when Benny and I were having a Happy Hour drink at an outdoor café in the Soulard neighborhood, Larry drove by in his Mini Cooper convertible, slowing to beep his horn and wave at me as he passed. "Holy shit," Benny had said. "Was that Mr. Potato Head?"

All three of Larry's qualities were on full display in my office that afternoon, although he seemed a tad intimidated by Jacki, especially at the outset of the meeting. She stood as he entered the conference room. Towering over Larry, she gave him a handshake that made his smile edge toward a grimace.

But he quickly recovered his swagger.

"Ladies," he said, chuckling as he leaned back in his chair and crossed his arms over his chest, "you claim malpractice?" A donkey bray, head thrown back. "All you have accomplished is royally pissing off my client, and believe me, ladies, that is one gal you don't want to royally piss off."

"Actually, Larry," I said, "that's good advice for you to follow in your dealings with Ms. Cross."

"Oh, Rachel, puh-leaze. Norma and I get along famously. She wants an attack dog, and that's my specialty." He bared his teeth. "Grrr!!"

Another donkey bray.

"Larry," I said, "have you read the property deed?"

"Of course I have."

"Do you understand the plaintiff's claim? How she seeks to invalidate that deed?"

"Rachel, I've read the pleadings. It's that spooky old Rule Against Perpetuities. Oooh. Be still my heart. You'll be sad to hear that I found a case that says the damn rule is so complicated that a lawyer can't be sued for malpractice for violating it."

"That's not Missouri law."

"True, but it's a helluva starting point, eh?"

"And a helluva ending point for you and your client," Jacki said.

Larry frowned. "What makes you say that?"

"As you should have already discovered," Jacki said, "Adam Fox knew that the deed violated the Rule Against Perpetuities before he had his client sign it."

Larry's eyes widened. "Actually knew?"

Jacki nodded.

"What do you base that on?"

"His own words."

"His own words? Where?"

"Here." I slid across the table a copy of that transcript of the last telephone conversation between Adam Fox and Irving Sliman.

Larry picked it up and read through it. He looked up at me. "I'm not seeing it."

"It's right before your eyes," I said. "You see where Adam says his concern is easy to resolve. He says to make the deed a trust. And then he cites a specific section of Chapter 456 of the Missouri Revised Statutes."

"Okay."

"Do you know what that section does?"

"Not yet."

"It provides a simple way to avoid the Rule Against Perpetuities in Missouri. All you need to do is set up a trust for the property and give the trustee the power to sell the property any time, including beyond the time period that would void the grant under the Rule Against Perpetuities. The section of the statute opens, and I quote, The Rule Against Perpetuities shall not apply to a trust, et cetera. Look what Adam says. He cites that section of the statute and then says it solves the issue."

"You get it, Larry?" Jacki asked. "Adam understood that the only issue that needed to be solved was the Rule Against Perpetuities. He understood the problem with the deed, and he had the solution."

Larry stared down at the transcript, now totally befuddled. "I don't understand."

"You don't understand what?" I said.

He gestured at the transcript. "Why didn't Sliman go along?"

"Maybe, just maybe, he wanted his client to have the ability to void that property deed at some later date."

"But..." Larry paused, trying to make sense out of it. "But if Adam knew there was that flaw in the deed, why did he... why did agree to it?"

"Read Danielle Knight's deposition," I said. "You'll see that her husband discovered during the divorce proceedings that Adam Fox was sleeping with Marsha Knight."

"Really? As in banging him?"

I nodded.

"My God." A donkey bray.

"You don't get it, do you?" I said.

Larry glanced between Jacki and me. "Get what?"

"If Jerry Knight told his wife, Danielle, that his ex-wife has been having an affair with her divorce lawyer, then guess who else knew that Marsha was sleeping with her lawyer?"

Larry frowned. "Danielle?"

"Yes. And who else?"

Larry frowned. "Is this some sort of trick question?"

I sighed. "Larry, think about it. You're the husband. You're going through a messy divorce. You and your lawyer are trying to find some edge, some leverage point. You discover that your soon-to-be ex-wife is having an affair with her divorce lawyer. Who would be the first person you would tell?"

Larry grinned. "Aha! I bet I know the answer to that one. Your lawyer. That's who you'd tell, right?"

I snuck a peek at Jacki, who rolled her eyes and shook her head.

"Correct, Larry," I said.

"So the old Slimeball knew, eh?"

"So it would seem."

"Now wait." Larry frowned. "Do you think he might have tried to use that information?"

"Read the transcript again Larry. And when you get to Adam Fox's reference to Rule 4-1.8, let me give you a hint. You have a pen?"

Larry pulled one out of the inner pocket of his suit jacket.

"Write this down," I said. "The Missouri Supreme Court Rules of Professional Conduct. Read them when you get back to your office. And when you're done, go back and read the rest of this transcript."

Larry scribbled down those citations and then looked up. "Okay. And then?"

I smiled. "And then you just might see a different pathway to defending the malpractice claim."

He nodded. A hesitant, puzzled nod—an unusual response from a man I'd never known to feel hesitant or puzzled. He must have sensed that himself, for his hesitant, puzzled nod slowly morphed into a chuckle and then, alas, a donkey bray as he got to his feet.

"Thank you, ladies. You've given me some good ammo. To quote the great late Jack Buck, 'We will see you tomorrow.'" He bowed toward me, and then toward Jacki. "Take care."

And then he left. A few seconds later, I heard him leave our offices.

"Jack Buck?" Jacki said.

I shrugged. "Whatever."

"What a bozo. But he's our grenade, eh?"

"Let's hope so."

"And we just pulled the pin?"

I smiled. "As Mad Max told me, cover your ears but keep your eyes peeled."

Section 4

"If you dig a pit for someone else,
you'll fall in it yourself."

—*Yiddish proverb*

Motion to Invalidate Mulligan Bloodline Trust Set for Hearing Before Circuit Judge Bauer

"We will reclaim the family legacy," declares Attorney Strauss

During his lifetime, Bert Mulligan gained acclaim as founder and CEO of The Mulligan Group. Two years after his death, he risks humiliation in a probate action disputing his status as the biological father of Carson Mulligan, born to Bert's second wife, Cyndi, eleven months after his death.

Under Mulligan's will, little Carson—as Mulligan's daughter—is sole heir to his stock in The Mulligan Group, purportedly valued at more than $100 million. But challenging her status as biological daughter is Bert Mulligan's biological son, the 53-year-old Bert Grimsley (né Mulligan), born during his father's first marriage.

"In science we trust," proclaimed Grimsley's trial attorney, Milton Strauss, referring to his theme for the hearing, scheduled to begin Monday morning before St. Louis County Circuit Judge Robert Bauer. "We may never know the identity of Carson's real father, but we will prove beyond a shadow of a doubt that Bert Mulligan is not her father. Ironically, we seek to uphold the integrity of the bloodline bequest, and in the process honor Bert Mulligan's true intent."

Carson Mulligan's lawyer, Rachel Gold, declined comment on the case or her opposing counsel's boast.

(CONTINUED ON PAGE 19)

Chapter Thirty-one

Milton Strauss went first, and, as I expected, kept it short and simple. His case began with the introduction into evidence of several uncontested documents, including Bert Mulligan's death certificate, his Last Will and Testament, and Carson Mulligan's birth certificate. Next was his reading into the record Cyndi Mulligan's interrogatory answers as to when she obtained the sperm deposits from Procreative Cryogenics and when she gave birth to Carson Mulligan. He followed that with a reading from the deposition testimony of George Luntz of Procreative Cryogenics concerning the lack of any records of sperm deposits under Bert Mulligan's Social Security number. He staged that reading as a dramatic recreation of the deposition, with a female paralegal named Suzie Bell reading my questions and a young male associate named John Something-or-other reading George Luntz's answers. Although it was hardly Shakespeare in the Park—Suzie's rendition made me sound like a gleeful nursery school teacher, and John lost his place three times, once actually reciting the next question instead of the preceding answer—the judge got the point. Indeed, he glanced over at me with a frown and then jotted something in his notebook.

Batting clean-up in the plaintiff's presentation was the plaintiff himself, Bert Grimsley. He strode to the witness stand, raised his right hand, nodded as the court reporter administered the oath, announced "I do" in a booming voice when she finished, nodded at the judge, took his seat, turned toward Strauss, who was standing at the podium, and put on what I assumed was his version of a game face.

Benny leaned close and whispered, "What a fucking douche-bag."

"Shush."

Strauss glanced down at his legal pad, cleared his throat, and looked up at Grimsley. "Please state your name for the record."

"Bertam Richard Grimsley."

"Is that how your name appears on your birth certificate?"

"No. I changed it a few years ago."

"What was your original name?"

"Bertram Richard Mulligan, Junior."

"Where did the Grimsley come from?"

"It is the maiden name of my beloved mother. I was honored to preserve it." He looked out in the courtroom, smiled at his mother, and turned back to his lawyer.

"I see," Strauss said. "And who are you, sir?"

Grimsley turned from Strauss to glare at Cyndi Mulligan, who was seated next to me. Cyndi lowered her head, and Grimsley shifted his stare to me. I gazed back, expressionless. After a moment, he gave me a sneer, turned back to Strauss, and in a loud voice answered, "I am the son, the only son, of Bertram Richard Mulligan. He was my father, he was married to my dear mother, and they were husband and wife at the time of her impregnation and at the time of my birth."

He turned toward me. "I—am—the—sole—biological—son—of—Bertram—Richard—Mulligan."

What followed that verbal thunderclap was, as Benny would later say, the courtroom equivalent of the aftermath of premature ejaculation. Strauss asked a series of open-ended questions— "Tell the Court about your education," "Tell the Court about your first job," "Tell the Court about your family," etc. Grimsley's responses were a rambling, increasingly flaccid, and largely irrelevant account of his life.

Thirty minutes into his testimony and it was clear that

Grimsley and Strauss had lost the interest of Judge Bauer, who appeared to be texting on his phone. I resisted the urge to object. When Strauss finally announced that he had no more questions for the witness, I scanned my notes, looked up at the judge, and checked my watch. It was five minutes to noon.

I stood. "Your Honor, I have some questions for Mr. Grimsley, but most are beyond the scope of the direct examination. Accordingly, to avoid objections from opposing counsel and in the interest of judicial efficiency, I respectfully request the right to reserve those questions until we call Mr. Grimsley in our case."

Judge Bauer glanced at his watch and then stared at Strauss. "I assume you have no problem with that, Counsel."

"Well," Strauss started, "if Miss Gold thinks she has some questions for my client, my feeling—"

"We're about to recess for lunch, Mr. Strauss. Do you have any more evidence to present?"

Strauss flipped through the notes on his legal pad, looked over at his client on the witness stand, and then back at the judge. "No, Your Honor. We believe we've provided more than sufficient evidence already. We are pleased to rest our case. But if Miss Gold has any questions—"

"Enough. Ms. Gold can ask your client her questions this afternoon. I will see you after lunch."

Judge Bauer rapped his gavel twice. "The Court will be in recess until one-thirty."

As the judge stood the bailiff announced, "All rise."

Chapter Thirty-two

Benny, Cyndi, and I went across the street to the St. Louis Bread Company for lunch. She listened as Benny and I went over our battle plans. At my request, Benny left for court a few minutes early to be there to greet our witnesses.

When he was gone, I turned to Cyndi. "There were three reporters in the courtroom this morning. And there's a Channel 5 News van parked out front of the courthouse. If this afternoon goes as planned, it'll be a hot topic in this town."

"Great." She shook her head wearily. "Just what I need."

"I know. Are you still okay with this?"

"I am." She sighed. "I'm doing this for Carson, not me."

"I know that, Cyndi." I reached across the table and took one of her hands in mine. "Are you still angry with him?"

She gazed at me, eyes clear. "Yes, I am definitely still pissed off."

She shook her head. "What a family. All of this. This should never have happened. That bloodline trust? He used me."

"I understand, Cyndi." I squeezed her hand. "One day at a time. Let's first get through this one."

She nodded. "I'll try."

"Remember, I'll ask you those simple questions, and you give me your simple answers. Don't let Strauss bait you on cross-examination. If he gets out of line—and he will—I'll object. But no matter what he asks, keep your answers short and to the point. Okay?"

She smiled. "Yes, boss."

And that's precisely what she did. My direct examination consisted of ten minutes of simple questions and simple answers, ending with this one:

"Since your husband's death, Mrs. Mulligan, have you had sexual relations with anyone?"

"No."

"No one?"

"No one."

I paused, pretending to glance down at my notes, allowing her answer to resonate.

I looked up at the judge. "No further questions, Your Honor."

Judge Bauer turned to Strauss. "Any cross, Counsel?"

Strauss chuckled as he got to his feet. "Oh, yes."

He tried to draw her out on cross-examination but got nowhere. Typical was the last series of questions and answers.

"Let me get this straight, ma'am. You expect us to believe you have had no sex with anyone else?"

"I do."

"Why should we believe you?"

"Because I loved my husband."

"That's all fine and good. But your husband is dead."

She stared at him.

"Well?" he finally said.

"Well what?"

"Your husband is dead."

I stood. "Objection, Your Honor. We will stipulate that Mrs. Mulligan's husband is dead. If Counsel has a question, he should ask it."

"Objection sustained." Judge Bauer turned to Strauss. "If you have another question, Counsel, then ask it."

Pause. "Nothing further."

Judge Bauer looked at me. "Ms. Gold?"

"Nothing further, Your Honor."

He turned to Cyndi. "You may step down, Mrs. Mulligan."

He looked back me. "Next witness."

Chapter Thirty-three

Benny stood. But for his ample girth and Jew-fro, he was almost unrecognizable in his blue pinstriped suit, white Oxford shirt, and blue-and-red striped tie.

He announced, "Defendant calls Dr. Robert Feldman."

Dr. Feldman was the fertility doctor who'd handled Cyndi's artificial insemination. He was a plump, soft-spoken man in his early sixties with a soothing manner.

Benny walked him through his relationship with Cyndi, from her first appointment to the day of Carson's delivery.

"The hospital notified me of the birth," Dr. Feldman said. "I came by later that afternoon to visit the new mother and her child."

"Is that your standard procedure?"

"Oh, yes." He smiled gently. "A successful pregnancy is a wonderful event in my practice."

He paused, cherishing the memory. "Mrs. Mulligan was crying. Tears of joy and tears of remembrance. It was February fourteenth. Valentine's Day. Cyndi told me that her little girl was a love child. Both for her and her late husband. It was a lovely moment, Counsel. Just lovely."

Benny let it linger for several seconds. In the silence of the courtroom I watched the judge's docket clerk dab her eyes with a tissue.

Benny resumed. "You have before you a set of documents marked as Defendant's Group Exhibit E. Do you recognize them?"

"I do. This is my patient file for Mrs. Mulligan. I maintain such a file for each of my patients."

"I see that the first several pages are your notes regarding Mrs. Mulligan's visits, beginning with the one you described earlier today."

"Yes," he said, studying the page. "This one here—these are the notes for her first visit. April eleventh. A little over a week after her husband's funeral."

"Page five of the notes covers your first attempt to artificially inseminate her, correct?"

"Yes. That attempt was not successful." He paged through the documents. "Here. Page seven. This concerns the second attempt, which was successful."

"On each of those pages, Doctor, you have recorded a series of letters and numbers that are labeled A.C. What is that?"

"Yes, A.C. That is the access code for the vials of frozen sperm I used. Certain sperm depositors provide sperm for a specific purpose, such as for use only with their wife, and thus they want to maintain control over their sperm. For those depositors, the sperm bank assigns a confidential access code. Such was the case here. Mrs. Mulligan told me that her late husband had provided her with that code, which she gave to me so that I could arrange for delivery of the correct vials of sperm."

Benny walked over to the blackboard. "Please read us the access code."

As the doctor read off the code, Benny wrote it down:

DG30WQSX973PMAK1

"Thank you, Doctor. Nothing further."

Judge Bauer turned to Strauss. "Counsel?"

"I have a few, Judge."

"Nicely done," I whispered to Benny when he returned to the table.

He gave me a wink. "Just teeing it up for you, boss. Almost show time."

Strauss flailed around for a few minutes before conceding to reality, namely, that trying to cross-examine the gentle but knowledgeable Dr. Robert Feldman on his area of expertise was as daunting as trying to cross-examine Mister Rogers on his neighborhood.

After Strauss took his seat, Judge Bauer said, "Any further witnesses, Ms. Gold?"

"Yes, Your Honor. Defendant recalls to the witness stand the plaintiff."

Bert Grimsley looked up from his notes with a frown. He glanced over at Strauss, who shrugged. Grimsley stood, buttoned his suit jacket, and strode over to the witness box.

As I approached the podium, I gazed at Bert Grimsley, who stared back at me from the witness stand with a smug grin.

"Good afternoon, Mr. Grimsley," I said.

"Same to you, Miss Gold."

"You understand that you are still under oath."

"I do."

"Have you ever had sexual relations with my client?"

Grimsley squinted. "Have I what?"

"Have you ever had sexual relations with my client?"

"Are you asking me whether I've banged your client?"

I turned to the judge. "Your Honor, could you please ask the witness to answer my question?"

Judge Bauer stared down at Grimsley, his face red. "Watch your language, sir. This is a court of law, not a fraternity house. Answer Counsel's question."

Grimsley looked back at me with a grin and shook his head. "No, Miss Gold. I have never had sexual relations with your client."

I looked down at my notes, pretending to study them.

I looked up. "Your attorney asked you several questions about your background—your education, the various jobs and titles you've held. If my notes are accurate, you have served as a member of the board of your church, correct?"

"That is correct."

"You also served one term on the board of the St. Louis Area Food Bank, correct?"

"Yep."

"Those aren't the only two boards you have served on over the years, correct?"

Grimsley squinted. "What do you mean?"

"Have you served on any other boards?"

He pursed his lips. "Maybe. I can't think of any others at the moment."

"Let me see if I can jog your memory. I did a Google search on you. It seems that a little over a decade ago you served a two-year term on the board of directors of the Testicular Cancer Society."

"Ah, yes. That's right."

"They held their annual fundraiser in St. Louis one of those two years, correct?"

"I believe you're right."

"You attended?"

"I sure did."

"Did The Mulligan Group buy a table for that event?"

"They certainly did."

"You were the General Counsel of The Mulligan Group at the time."

"I was also vice president.

"Did your father attend that event?"

His smile vanished. In a terse voice he said, "I don't recall."

"What caused you to become active in that organization back then?"

"They do good work."

"Did you have a more personal connection?"

"What do you mean?"

"Are you a survivor of testicular cancer, Mr. Grimsley?"

"As a matter of fact, I am." He leaned forward, eyes narrowing. "Why do you ask?"

"Actually, Mr. Grimsley, I'm the one who asks the questions in this proceeding. You are not presently married, are you, sir?"

"Not presently."

"You are divorced, correct?"

"So what?"

I turned to the judge, who needed no prompting.

"Watch that tone, Mr. Grimsley." Judge Bauer's nostrils flared. "Just answer the question."

Grimsley squinted at me. "Yes, I am divorced."

"Do you have any children?"

"Not yet."

"At the time you were diagnosed with testicular cancer, Mr. Grimsley, did you take any precautionary measures to preserve your future potential as a father?"

He stared at me. "Such as?"

"Such as any measures. You heard my client testify that your father took precautionary measures. Did you, as well?"

He crossed his arms over his chest. "Don't you think that's a personal question?"

"Do you?"

"I view it as a brazen invasion of my privacy."

I gazed at him. I knew the judge was waiting for me to ask that the witness be instructed to answer, waiting to order him to do so.

After a long pause, I said, "I certainly didn't mean to offend you, sir. Are you telling us that you would prefer not to answer that question in open court?"

"Yes, I am."

I turned to the judge. "May I approach the witness, Your Honor?"

Judge Bauer, clearly baffled, nodded. "You may."

I walked over and handed Grimsley a sheet of paper and a pen.

After returning to the podium, I said, "Mr. Grimsley, you have made it clear that there are certain details of your life you do not want to share in open court. I assume that one of those details is your Social Security number."

He snorted. "I should say so."

"Then please print your Social Security number on the sheet of paper I just handed to you, along with your name. Once you have done so, hand it to the courtroom clerk, who will mark it as Defendant's Exhibit F and give it to the judge for safekeeping. Okay?"

Grimsley gave me a puzzled squint. "You want me to do what?"

I turned to the court reporter. "Could you please read the witness my last question?"

After she did, Strauss stood. "I object, Your Honor. This is nonsensical. Completely irrelevant."

Judge Bauer turned to me, his eyebrows raised. "Counsel?"

"I respectfully ask for the Court's indulgence. I will demonstrate its relevance before I rest our case. Should I fail to do so, the Court may tear up the exhibit."

The judge nodded. "Okay, Ms. Gold. We'll give you a little leeway here, but you better deliver."

"Thank you, Your Honor."

The judge turned to Strauss. "Objection noted, Counsel. I will hold off ruling on the matter until opposing counsel rests her case." He looked at Grimsley. "Do you understand Ms. Gold's request?"

"I guess so."

"Then do it."

"Okay."

When he finished, he handed the paper to the judge's clerk, who added the exhibit sticker and handed it up to Judge Bauer, who looked at the paper, frowned, and set it down next to his gavel.

"Mr. Grimsley," I said, "the clerk just marked that sheet of paper as Defendant's Exhibit F. For the record, sir, what did you write on Exhibit F?"

"Exactly what you told me to write."

"And what was that, sir?"

He rolled his eyes. "My—name—and—my—Social—Security—number."

"Thank you, Mr. Grimsley. I have no further questions."

"Mr. Strauss?"

Strauss chuckled and shook his head. "No questions, Your Honor."

"You may step down, sir."

After Grimsley returned to his seat at counsel's table next to Milton Strauss, the judge said, "Well, Ms. Gold, I assume you have more."

I smiled. "I do, Your Honor. One final witness."

"Very good. Let's proceed."

I nodded toward Benny, who stood and walked toward the back of the courtroom. Other than the parties themselves, the judge had ordered all witnesses to remain outside the courtroom until called to testify.

When Benny reached the courtroom door, I said, "Defendant calls Donald Reynolds."

Benny opened the door and gestured toward someone in the hallway.

Chapter Thirty-four

Donald Reynolds was the CEO of Unisource Laboratories. Tall, slender, and athletic, he was in his sixties with thinning gray hair neatly trimmed and combed. He had on a dark blue suit, crisp white shirt, a red patterned tie, and freshly shined cordovan cap-toe shoes. His strong, angular features were lightly tanned, no doubt from his twice-weekly golf games at Bellerive Country Club.

"How long have you been the CEO of Unisource, Mr. Reynolds?"

"Twenty-two years, Ms. Gold. It will be twenty-three next month."

"So you were at Unisource when it was acquired by The Mulligan Group?"

"I was."

"Were you CEO at the time?"

"I was."

"And thus you knew and worked with Bertram Mulligan for nearly two decades."

"That is a correct. He was a fine gentlemen and an outstanding businessman. A tough and crafty man, both in and out of the boardroom."

"Crafty?"

Reynolds laughed. "Oh, yes, Ms. Gold. Bert loved challenges. He used to tell me that there was no such thing as a problem that couldn't be solved."

"How would you describe your relationship with Mr. Mulligan."

"Excellent. I had great respect for the gentleman."

"One of Unisource's divisions is Procreative Cryogenics, correct?"

"That's true. Procreative has been a division of ours since before I joined the company."

"One of the services provided by Procreative Cryogenics is the freezing and storage of human sperm deposits, correct?"

"That is correct, Ms. Gold."

I paused to allow Judge Bauer to absorb that information before moving on.

"Mr. Reynolds, did Mr. Mulligan ever have a conversation with you regarding his own sperm deposits?"

Reynolds smiled. "He did. He approached me regarding that subject approximately a year before he passed away."

"Tell us about it."

"Objection," Strauss said. "Hearsay."

Judge Bauer looked at me. "Ms. Gold?"

"Your Honor, this is merely background for the actual evidence we will be introducing. Just a few questions to provide the Court with some helpful context for that evidence. I would urge the Court to allow Mr. Reynolds to testify with the understanding that the Court can determine for itself the relevance, reliability, and admissibility of that testimony."

Judge Bauer nodded. "Objection noted. You may answer, Mr. Reynolds."

"Bert and I were having lunch at his club—St. Louis Country Club. Just the two of us. I knew there was something personal on his mind."

"How did you know that?"

"Bert and I had many business lunches over the years, and for those his secretary would call mine to make the arrangements. Typically, we met in the conference room adjoining his office, or occasionally at the Missouri Athletic Club. But this time Bert called me himself, and when I got to his club, I discovered that we were having lunch in a private room. Just the two of us."

"Were you right about the personal nature of the lunch?"

"Oh, yes. He started off telling me he had something personal and confidential to discuss. He told me that he and his new wife had been trying without success to conceive a child. He'd undergone tests and learned that he had a low sperm court. Not that unusual for a man of his age, but unfortunate for one trying to conceive a baby."

Strauss stood. "Objection, more hearsay."

The judge turned to me. "Counsel?"

"Your Honor, Mr. Mulligan's low sperm count has already been confirmed by the affidavit we submitted from his urologist, Dr. Silverman. Mr. Strauss did not object to that affidavit."

The judge nodded. "Overruled. You may continue." He turned to Strauss. "There is no jury, Counsel. As before, I will allow this testimony for what it's worth, and you can have a continuing objection. Continue, Ms. Gold."

I turned back to Reynolds. "You were describing your conversation with Mr. Mulligan about his low sperm count."

"Yes. Bert told me that about ten years earlier, as a precautionary matter for that very situation, he had made some sperm deposits with Procreative Cryogenics. His problem was that he had misplaced the access code for those deposits. He was quite embarrassed by that."

"Why?"

Reynolds smiled. "Bert Mulligan was a highly organized individual, and he demanded that of others as well. He saw this misplacement of the access code as a humiliating blunder on his part, even an early sign of senility. I reassured him that he was hardly the first sperm donor to lose his access code. I told him that if he gave me his Social Security number, I was sure we could locate his sperm deposits and his access code."

"How did he react?"

"He was relieved—and grateful. He wrote down his Social Security number and made me promise to keep it all confidential.

He specifically requested that I handle the matter entirely on my own and not delegate the task to anyone else."

"Is that what you did?"

"Absolutely. When I got back to the office, I personally logged onto the Procreative Cryogenics computer and performed the data search myself."

D.F.W.B., I said to myself.

I asked, "Was your search successful?"

"It was. Within an hour I had the pleasure of calling him with his access code."

Reynolds looked over at Cyndi and smiled. "I was privileged to play a small role in that happy event, Mrs. Mulligan."

Cyndi did not smile back.

"Mr. Reynolds," I said, "have you brought with you today your company's business records regarding those sperm deposits?"

"I have. I printed them out myself."

I turned to the judge. "May I approach the witness?"

"You may."

I walked over to the witness box and handed Donald Reynolds a stapled set of documents. "Mr. Reynolds, I have handed you a set of documents marked as Defendant's Exhibit G. Do you recognize them?"

He flipped through the documents. "Yes."

"Are those the business records you brought with you today?"

"Yes."

I turned toward Benny and nodded. He took a copy of the exhibit out of a folder and handed it to Milton Strauss.

I turned back to the witness. "Would you please read aloud the access code for those three sperm deposits?"

All eyes turned toward the blackboard as Reynolds read off the same combination of numbers and letters that were already on the blackboard.

"What is the name identified with that access code?"

"It says here 'Mulligan, B.'"

"How many vials were listed under that access code?"

"Three."

"Do the records indicate what happened with those vials?"

"Yes. A Doctor Robert A. Feldman obtained one vial for Mrs. Mulligan two years ago on April 29th. The following month— May 31st, to be exact—he obtained the other two vials."

"Your Honor," I said, "can I have a moment to confer with my co-Counsel?"

"Make it quick, Ms. Gold."

I walked over to the table where Benny and Cyndi were seated.

I leaned in close to Benny. "Well?" I whispered. "Should I?"

Benny glanced over at Strauss, who was grinning and nodding as he examined the several-page exhibit. "Looks to me like he's going to do it for you."

I turned toward Strauss and then back at Benny. "You think?"

"Look at him now. He's got the subpoena you served on the sperm bank. Showing it to Grimsley. That knucklehead thinks he's Perry Mason. I say we sit back and watch him blow up his lawsuit."

"Counsel?" Judge Bauer said.

I stood, my mind racing. I'd already put in all the evidence we needed. Assuming Strauss tried to cross-examine Reynolds but avoided the land mine, I could trigger it on redirect. And if he decided not to cross-examine Reynolds, I could still connect the dots in closing argument.

I glanced over at Strauss, who was grinning as he jotted down notes.

Why not?

I turned to the judge. "Nothing further, Your Honor."

"Mr. Strauss?"

"Oh, yeah, Judge." Strauss chuckled, setting down his pen. "I got a few."

"Proceed."

Strauss took the exhibit, stepped to the podium, and turned to Reynolds with a predatory grin.

"Mr. Reynolds," he started, "are you aware that earlier in this lawsuit Miss Gold served a subpoena on your company? That subpoena sought the very same records you have brought with you today."

"Really?"

"In fact, let me show you a copy of that subpoena. It's Plaintiff's Exhibit 1."

He handed it to Reynolds, who glanced through it and then looked up. "Okay."

"You see there that it seeks all records regarding any sperm deposits by Mr. Mulligan, correct?"

"I do."

"It even has his Social Security number, doesn't it?"

"That's what the document indicates."

"Are you aware that your company produced no documents in response to that subpoena?"

"Is that so?"

Strauss smiled. "Oh, yes, sir. That is most certainly so."

Reynolds frowned. "I didn't realize that."

"My, my. Well, how about we take a look at the Social Security number in the subpoena?"

"I see it."

Strauss walked over to the chalkboard. "How about reading off that number? The one in the subpoena?"

As Reynolds read the nine-digit number, Strauss wrote it onto the chalkboard.

"This number you just read from the subpoena—" Strauss paused to point at the chalkboard "—is indeed the late Mr. Mulligan's actual Social Security number. We have confirmed that from other personal records of his, including the tax returns."

"Okay."

"You understand what that means?"

Reynolds shook his head. "No."

"That means your company has absolutely no record of any sperm deposit ever made by a person with that Social Security number. None, sir. Zero. Zilch. Okay?"

Reynolds gave him a puzzled look. "Mr. Mulligan gave me his Social Security number. He wrote it down."

"Ah." Strauss grinned. "Mr. Mulligan gave you *a* Social Security number, sir. Did you ever confirm that the number he gave you was in fact *his* Social Security number?"

Reynolds rubbed his chin. "I don't recall."

"Let me direct your attention back to the documents you brought with you today. The ones Miss Gold marked as Exhibit G. You feel pretty confident in the accuracy of those records?"

"Yes, I do. We have high standards for our data."

"Excellent answer, Mr. Reynolds. How about we take a look at the Social Security number on those records? I think you'll find it on page four."

"Yes, I see it."

"Good. Now take a look at the number up here on the chalkboard—the one you just read aloud from the subpoena."

Reynolds looked at the chalkboard and then down at the records.

Strauss was grinning. "They aren't the same number, are they?"

Reynolds looked at the chalkboard again, and then down at the records. "You are correct." He looked up at Strauss. "They are different."

"Yes, I am correct." Strauss walked over to the chalkboard and picked up the chalk. "Okay, Mr. Reynolds. For the record, how about reading aloud the Social Security number from the documents you printed out this morning? The Social Security number that is actually connected to the vials of sperm your company delivered to Dr. Feldman—to the vials of sperm of the actual father of the defendant's child. Do it nice and slow, sir, so I can write it down."

Reynolds got as far as the sixth digit when Grimsley jumped to his feet and shouted, "Stop!"

The courtroom was silent. Strauss turned to his client wide-eyed, the chalk still in his hand. Judge Bauer stared at Grimsley. Benny stifled a laugh.

Strauss said, "A moment, Your Honor."

He hurried over to Grimsley. As they huddled in frenzied conversation, I looked up at Judge Bauer. He had lifted the sheet of paper from earlier today, the one where Grimsley had written down his own Social Security number. The judge looked at the paper and then at the blackboard and then back at the paper. He leaned back in his chair, his lips pursed. He folded his arms over his chest and glanced at me. I nodded.

Strauss stepped back to the podium. Grimsley was slumped in his chair, eyes down, slowly shaking his head.

"Uh, Your Honor," Strauss stammered.

"What is it now, Counsel?"

"My client has, uh, he has decided to dismiss this lawsuit."

Judge Bauer studied him. "Just to be clear, Mr. Strauss, at issue in this lawsuit is the trust established for the benefit of any child born into the decedent's bloodline. You propose to dismiss your challenge with respect to the child named Carson Sue Mulligan, born to defendant on February fourteenth of last year?"

"Yes, Your Honor."

"Thus your client no longer disputes the claim that the child named Carson Sue Mulligan, born to defendant on February fourteenth of last year was indeed born into the decedent's bloodline, correct?"

Strauss took a deep breath and exhaled. "Correct."

Bauer lifted his gavel, looked over at me, then back at Strauss. "Case dismissed."

Bang.

Section 5

"No one sees the hump on his own back."

—Yiddish proverb

ST. LOUIS LAWYER WEEKLY (NOVEMBER 9)

BATTLE OF THE KNIGHTS GOES TO TRIAL
Outcome Likely to Turn
on Obscure Rule of Property

A mysterious rule dating back to the Middle Ages and notoriously difficult to apply properly may determine the outcome of a property bequest at the heart of a legal battle between the two wives of the late Jerome Knight. The case is set for trial Monday before Circuit Court Judge Harry Ballsack.

Knight's widow, Danielle Knight, seeks an order invalidating a life estate granted to Knight's ex-wife Marsha in Fontainebleau Estates, the luxury high-rise apartment complex in Clayton. Danielle's claim is that the grant, part of the divorce proceedings, violates the Rule Against Perpetuities. She is represented by Thomas Sterling of Abbott & Windsor. Marsha Knight's attorney is Rachel Gold of Gold & Brand. Both attorneys declined to comment on the case.

Earlier in the fall, Gold ratcheted up the stakes by adding the Cross Law Firm to the case, alleging malpractice in its representation of Marsha Knight in the divorce proceeding, including its approval of the property bequest now at issue.

The law firm's principal, Norma Cross, had no hesitance in commenting on the allegations against her firm. "Rachel Gold will rue the day she filed this pathetic claim against my firm. Once we get it thrown out of court, we'll come after her with a vengeance seeking sanctions."

Her firm is represented by Lawrence Blatz. Informed of his client's comments, he laughed and said, "Ditto that."

(CONTINUED ON PAGE 12)

old school," but he was also brilliant and articulate. Despite
three bursts of tough, probing questions by Jacki, he was unable
to expose a crack in his opinion.

Chapter Thirty-five

Jacki and I spent most of Sunday mapping out our trial strategy.
Our options were limited.

On the previous Friday, the parties had exchanged their "Will
Call" witness lists, *i.e.*, the witnesses they intended to call at trial.
The plaintiff's list confirmed what I had assumed would be Tom
Sterling's trial strategy: keep it simple. He listed two witnesses:
his client and Hiram McAllister. Neither was a surprise.

Presumably, Sterling envisioned Danielle Knight's principal
role, at least for the purpose of his direct examination, to attach
a pretty young face to the name on the lawsuit caption. I had
other plans for her.

As for Hiram McAllister, he was the plaintiff's expert witness.
Now in his late sixties, McAllister was a distinguished professor at
St. Louis University Law School and the co-author of *McAllister
and Christianson on Property Law*. His written expert witness
report concluded as follows: "Accordingly, my opinion is that
the real property deed at issue in the case so blatantly violates the
Rule Against Perpetuities in Missouri that it was void *ab initio*."

While that was an opinion that might have some value in our
malpractice claim against the Cross Law Firm, it created a daunting barrier to scale in our attempt to refute the plaintiff's claim
that the deed was void. Jacki had taken Professor McAllister's
deposition a month ago. I'd watched it later on the video. The
silver-haired McAllister was pompous and aloof and decidedly

"old school," but he was also brilliant and articulate. Despite three hours of tough, probing questions by Jacki, she was unable to expose even a crack in his opinion.

The more intriguing witness list was the one Larry Blatz had submitted for his client, the Cross Law Firm. Norma Cross was on the list, of course. As was Daniel Crocker, a lawyer who Blatz was going to try to get the judge to allow to testify as an expert witness on the question of legal malpractice. I'd taken a pass on deposing Crocker after doing a little digging into his credentials—unimpressive—and his social network, where, among other things, he and Blatz were Facebook friends. Rather than give him a dress rehearsal of my cross-examination during a deposition—and thus give him an opportunity to concoct a new, less flawed version of his testimony for court—I decided to save my questions for the trial. My first strategy, however, was to get the judge to disqualify him as an expert.

The other name on Blatz's witness list was more intriguing: Adam Fox's sister, Shannon McCarthy. As I learned when I called her later that day, she was now a hostile witness.

"I can't believe it," she'd said, her voice lace with anger. "You're accusing my dear dead brother of malpractice. The nerve!"

Before I could respond she hung up.

My Will Call witness was short: just three names. The first was Marsha Knight. The second was Phoebe Hecht, the Washington University professor who taught property law and would serve as my expert witness in the malpractice claim against the Cross Law Firm. My third witness, also an expert, was Robert Dunlop, a commercial real estate appraiser. He would testify that the present value of the life estate granted to Marsha under the property deed—and thus the value of her loss if that deed was invalidated—was $5.2 million. His purpose, in short, was to attach a dollar amount to Marsha's malpractice claims against the Cross Law Firm.

Judge Ballsack's pre-trial order required disclosure of only the "will call" witness lists, and not the "may call" list that some other judges require. And thus each party no doubt had a few surprise witnesses that, depending upon how their case went, might get called to the stand.

Marsha Knight arrived at our office at seven p.m. that Sunday. Jacki and I went over her testimony for a couple of hours. We'd probably have another opportunity to work with her Monday night, since she was unlikely to take the witness stand on that first day.

I walked her out to her car.

"One last thing, Marsha."

She turned. "What?"

"Dressing for court. It may seem a little frivolous, but I promise it's not."

She frowned. "Okay."

"Optics are important in the courtroom, even when it's just a judge. We need to make sure he understands the consequences to you if you lose. One way to do that is through what you wear. No flashy jewelry. Easy on the makeup. No heels. And keep your clothes simple. A skirt and blouse, a dress, or a pantsuit—but nothing flashy. Okay?"

She nodded. "I understand."

"Good." I smiled. "Now go home and get a good night's sleep. Hopefully, you spend tomorrow as a spectator."

"I sure hope so."

"Goodnight, Marsha."

"Goodnight, Rachel."

Chapter Thirty-six

Before the first day of trial, every good lawyer talks to the client about optimal courtroom attire—and Tom Sterling's discussion with Danielle Knight had obviously been different than mine with Marsha Knight. I had assumed, perhaps naively, that the Danielle Knight who would take the witness stand that first day would be the demure but competent ICU nurse. Instead, we got the flashy "beautiful people" version, the one with a smile as dazzling as her jewelry, the one that appears in the photos in the *Ladue News* and the other society magazines from the prior week's charity fundraiser events. This version strutted into the courtroom in high heels with coiffed red hair, a deep tan, gold earrings and matching necklace, and a snug navy jacquard dress that highlighted her long legs and big boobs.

I would have taken a different tack. After all, Danielle was seeking to grab back the entire property settlement that her late husband had given to his first wife—and in the process, as Tom Sterling surely knew I would emphasize, leave that first wife impoverished. But then again, I'm not a guy, and Tom Sterling certainly is. And little Harry Ballsack's slack-jawed reaction as Danielle sashayed up to the witness stand seemed to affirm Sterling's concept of optimal courtroom attire for his client.

Nevertheless, once she'd been sworn in and taken her seat, Danielle performed her role with calm composure as Sterling walked her through nearly two hours of direct examination—her background, her profession, her marriage to Jerry Knight, her widowhood, and her "reluctant" decision to challenge the property deed at issue.

When we returned to the courtroom after the lunch break and Danielle resumed her seat in the witness box, Sterling stepped back to the podium, gestured toward Marsha Knight, who was seated at counsel table between Jacki and me.

"Danielle," he said, "one final question: are you motivated today by any ill will toward the defendant?"

"Oh, no. Not at all." She turned to the judge. "I have no hard feelings toward Mrs. Knight. This is not personal. Not in the least."

Judge Ballsack smiled and nodded at her.

"I have no further questions, Your Honor."

Ballsack turned to me. "Counsel?"

I stood. "I have some questions for the witness."

"Proceed."

I stepped to the podium. "Hello, Mrs. Knight."

She gave me a forced, "Hello."

"No hard feelings toward my client? Did I hear that correctly?"

She stiffened slightly. "Yes."

"What's your net worth, Mrs. Knight?"

She shrugged. "I don't know."

"I've reviewed your late husband's probate file. According to the public filings, you inherited money, stock, and property worth more than forty million dollars, correct?"

She shrugged again. "Maybe."

I held up a stack of probate court filings and turned to Sterling. "Counsel, these are certified copies of the probate court records. I can go through the lengthy process of having these records admitted into evidence or you can save us all some time and just stipulate that your client inherited more than forty million dollars from her late husband."

Sterling stood and looked toward the judge. "No need to waste the Court's valuable time. We will so stipulate, Your Honor. And we will also object as to the relevance of this evidence."

Ballsack turned to me. "Counsel?"

"Impeachment, Your Honor. The plaintiff claims her lawsuit is not motivated by any ill will toward my client even though if she succeeds she will leave my client destitute and in the poor house. Now if the plaintiff herself were impoverished, if she were struggling to make ends meet, perhaps living on food stamps, and thus had a legitimate financial need to grab back this property, her claim of no ill will might be credible. But if she is worth more than forty million dollars, with homes here and in Aspen, Colorado, and in Naples, Florida, then I think the Court can see no motivation for this vicious lawsuit other than her ill will toward my client."

Sterling was on his feet. "I object to that mischaracterization of the Widow Knight, Your Honor."

Ballsack banged his gavel. "Enough! Enough from both you. If you have any other questions for this witness, Ms. Gold, ask them now."

I spent the next thirty minutes poking around and pecking away at some of her earlier testimony, but mostly for the purpose of getting her into a sufficiently irritated state for my final series of questions.

"During your marriage to Mr. Knight," I said, "he talked to you about his first wife, my client, correct?"

"We talked about many things."

"I'm sure you did, Mrs. Knight. But that's not what I asked. Listen to the question. Did he talk to you about my client?"

"Yes."

"And he talked to you about the divorce, correct?"

"Yes."

"And he talked to you about my client's divorce lawyer, correct?"

"I guess so."

"In fact, he told you that my client was having sex with her divorce lawyer during the divorce proceeding, correct?"

"Objection. Irrelevant and inflammatory and prejudicial."

Ballsack glared at me. "Counsel?"

"May we approach?"

The judge sighed. "Fine. Approach."

Sterling and I stepped over to the far side of the judge's bench—the side opposite the witness box.

"What is it?" Ballsack asked.

"This is highly relevant, Your Honor," I said in a whisper, "and opposing Counsel knows that it is. It's relevant to this claim and, moreover, it's highly relevant to our malpractice claim against the Cross Law Firm. I only have a few more questions in this line of inquiry if this Court will allow me to continue. Otherwise, I would request that the Court take a recess so that I can fully explain this outside the hearing of the witness and make an offer of proof for the record on appeal."

Ballsack stared at me. "Just a few more questions?"

I nodded. "Ten minutes at most."

"Fine. Get it over with."

I walked back to the podium and Tom Sterling returned to his counsel table.

I turned to Danielle, who was clearly angry. "To repeat my last question, Mrs. Knight, your husband told you that my client was having sex with her divorce lawyer during the divorce proceeding, correct?"

"Sex? I don't remember that."

"You don't remember that he told you his ex-wife was having sex with her divorce lawyer?"

"No."

"Mrs. Knight, do you recall that I took your deposition earlier in this case?"

"Yes."

"In fact, the court reporter sent your lawyer a copy of your deposition transcript for you to review for accuracy, correct?"

"Maybe, I'm not sure."

"May I approach the witness, Your Honor?"

"Fine."

"Let me hand you a copy of that transcript, Mrs. Knight." I turned toward the judge's clerk. "And here is an extra copy for the Court."

She handed it up to the judge.

I went back to the podium. "Turn to page 243, Mrs. Knight."

I waited.

She looked up. "Okay."

"It's the last page of the transcript. The heading reads 'Certification,' correct?"

"Yes."

"Please read aloud the language below that heading."

"Okay." She cleared her throat. "'I, the undersigned, do hereby certify that I have read the foregoing deposition and that, to the best of my knowledge, said deposition is true and accurate with the exception of the following corrections listed below.'"

"And are there any corrections listed below?"

"No."

"Is there a handwritten date and signature below that certification?"

"Yes."

"Whose signature is that?"

"Mine."

"So you read your deposition transcript on that date and certified that to the best of your knowledge it was true and accurate, correct?"

"Yes. Yes. Yes."

"Thank you. Now earlier I asked you whether your husband told you that his ex-wife was having sex with her divorce lawyer and you said you didn't remember, correct?"

"Yes."

"Let's see if we can refresh your memory. Please turn to page 187 of your deposition."

I waited as she found the page and the judge found the page.

"Now, for context, please read aloud your answer, which starts at line seven."

She looked up, eyes wide. "You want me to read that?"

"Yes, we're trying to refresh your memory. Perhaps this passage will help. Read it, please."

She stared down at the page for a moment, took a deep breath, and read aloud: "How about, uh, um, screwing your own lawyer, lady? In your own, uh, expletive, uh, home? While your teenage daughter's bedroom is just down the hall?"

She looked up.

"Continue," I said.

She looked over at Sterling and then back down at the transcript. "Your client has no shame," she read. "She deserves exactly what's going to happen to her in this lawsuit."

"Good. And then I asked you 'How do you know that?' and at line 22 you ask, 'How do I know what?' and I said, 'That my client was sleeping with her divorce lawyer.' And what's your answer? It's at the top of the next page—page 188."

That next line in the transcript read: *Sleeping? You mean fucking like two rabbits in heat?*

She looked down at the transcript and then up at her lawyer and then over at the judge, whose facial expression confirmed that he had just read that line.

She said, "Do I have to read that out loud?"

"Yes," I said. "We're trying to refresh your memory."

Danielle shook her head. "Okay, okay, I remember now. My husband told me that your client was having sex with her divorce lawyer."

"So this is a fact that your husband knew, correct?"

"I guess so."

"And did he tell you how he found out that my client was having sex with her divorce lawyer?"

"Objection," Sterling said. "That conversation is protected by the spousal privilege."

I turned to the judge. "Perhaps it was protected once upon a time, Your Honor. But as you see from the transcript, she voluntarily waived that privilege."

"Objection overruled. The witness can answer."

Danielle just sat there, eyes wide.

"Mrs. Knight?" I said. "I asked you how your husband found out that my client was having sex with her divorce lawyer. The judge says you can answer that."

"He saw them."

"He saw them having sex?"

"No, I mean, he saw her lawyer coming out of her house early one morning."

"Okay. And what else did he see that morning?"

"The lawyer was dressed, but she was in her nightgown. He saw them kiss in the driveway."

"And he saw this before the divorce was final?"

She frowned. "I think so."

"Did he tell you that he told his lawyer what he saw?"

"Objection, Your Honor. This is clearly covered by the spousal privilege."

"Sustained. Move on, Counsel."

I looked down at my notes and then back at the witness. "Mrs. Knight, you have no legal training, correct?"

"Correct."

"Never taken a course in property law, correct?"

"Correct."

"I assume you could not explain to me the Rule Against Perpetuities."

She laughed. "You assume correctly."

"Then how did you know to hire a lawyer to challenge this deed under the Rule Against Perpetuities?"

"Objection. Attorney-client privilege."

"Sustained."

"Leaving aside the Rule Against Perpetuities, how did you know to hire a lawyer to challenge the deed?"

"Objection. Attorney-client privilege."

"Sustained."

"Did your husband tell you that he and his lawyer had made sure that the deed was defective and that you could challenge it?"

"Objection. Spousal privilege."

"Sustained."

I hadn't expected to get an answer to those last questions. The goal was to plant the questions in the judge's mind in the hope that he might provide himself with the answers.

I smiled. "Thank you, Mrs. Knight. No further questions, Your Honor."

Judge Ballsack said, "Anything further, Mr. Sterling?"

Sterling flipped through his notes, stood, and shook his head. "Nothing further, Your Honor."

Judge Ballsack turned to Danielle. "Thank you, Mrs. Knight. You may—"

"—Time out!"

We all turned.

Larry Blatz was standing and making a time-out sign with his hands. "Got a few more questions for the lovely lady, Judge."

Ballsack frowned, leaned back in his chair, and shook his head. "Then ask them, Mr. Blatz."

Blatz chuckled as he stepped up the podium. "Thanks, Judge."

I glanced over at Jacki. She raised her eyebrows and shrugged.

Blatz obviously had his own vision of optimal courtroom attire, which today featured a plaid sports jacket, green slacks, and an enormous red-and-white polka-dot bow tie.

"According to my notes, Mrs. Knight," he said, looking down at his legal pad, "you are not able to explain to us the Rule Against Perpetuities. Is that an accurate statement?"

"Yes."

"Pretty complex stuff, eh?"

"I suppose."

"And not just you, eh?"

"Pardon?"

"You're not the only one who thinks it pretty complex stuff, right?"

"Objection." Sterling stood. "The question is vague and lacks foundation."

"Sustained. Be more specific, Counsel."

"No problema. Your lawyer thinks it's pretty complex stuff, right?"

"Objection. Attorney-client privilege."

"Sustained. Get to the point, Mr. Blatz."

"You have any friends who are lawyers?"

Danielle paused as she thought it over. "Yes, a few."

"Ever ask any of them about their opinion on the Rule Against Perpetuities?"

"Objection. Irrelevant."

"Sustained."

"Any of those lawyers ever tell you it's a pretty doggone complicated rule?"

"Objection. Hearsay and irrelevant."

"Sustained!" Ballsack banged his gavel. "Move on, Counsel. Or just sit down."

Blatz chuckled. "I think I've more than made my point, Judge. Nothing further here. Over and out."

The look Norma Cross gave him as he returned to their table seemed the perfect illustration for that saying, *If looks could kill.*

Blatz was not her choice of attorneys. But since he'd been retained by her malpractice insurance carrier, she was stuck with him. Rarely have I felt such tender affection for an insurance company.

"Thank you, Mrs. Knight," the judge said. "You may now step down from the stand."

Ballsack checked his watch and turned to Sterling. "Call your next witness."

"You Honor, the plaintiff calls Professor Hiram McAllister."

Chapter Thirty-seven

In addition to Hiram McAllister's obvious qualifications as an expert witness in the case, a more subtle but important qualification emerged during the first few minutes of Tom Sterling's direct examination.

"Professor, for how long have you taught property law at the St. Louis University Law School?"

"This fall marks my fortieth year, Mr. Sterling."

"Four decades. My goodness, sir. Well done."

McAllister smiled. "Thank you."

With his shock of white hair, bushy white eyebrows, ruddy complexion, and brown tweed sports jacket, McAllister seemed Central Casting's answer to a call for an esteemed emeritus professor of law.

"I understand that many of your former students have become prominent figures in our local and national bar."

"That is true, Mr. Sterling. My goal as their teacher was to prepare them for the rigors of the legal world, and I must say that I have been most pleased with the results of my efforts. Several of my former students have become senior partners in law firms, both here and elsewhere, including three managing partners over the years. More than two dozen of my former students are now professors in their own right at law schools here and around the country, including Stanford, Michigan, and Harvard. And I am proud to count among my former students more than twenty federal and state court judges, including, I might add—" and he paused to smile at Judge Ballsack "—the presiding judge in this case. You were a good student, Harry."

Ballsack blushed and shrugged. "But not good enough for an A."

McAllister chuckled. "Not many were, Harry. Not many. Getting a B in my class is something to be proud of."

I leaned close to Jacki. "Give Tom points for picking the right expert."

"Might help us, though."

Over the next hour of testimony, McAllister walked the Court through the history, the purpose, and the operation of the Rule Against Perpetuities. It was an eye-glazing journey until he reached the property deed at issue, which Sterling presented in blown-up form as a large poster that he placed on an easel facing the judge at an angle between the witness box and the empty jury box. McAllister stood by the easel with a yellow highlighter marker in his hand and moved sentence by sentence through the document, highlighting each of its defects.

"In short," he stated after resuming his seat in the witness box, "Exhibit One is a tour de force of violations of the Rule Against Perpetuities."

"Thank you, Professor. I have nothing further."

Judge Ballsack turned to our table.

Jacki rose. "A few questions, Your Honor."

The judge grinned and raised his arms in a welcoming gesture. "Ah, Miss Brand. Please proceed."

I lowered my head to hide my smile. Jacki, God bless her, was the Helen of Troy for more than one of the older and shorter judges in this town. Out in the St. Louis County Courthouse, Judge Howard Flinch was one of at least three judges smitten by my six-foot three-inch, two-hundred-fifty-pound high-heeled law partner, dressed today in a navy pantsuit, white blouse, and low heels. And here in the Civil Courthouse in downtown St. Louis, for reasons too obscure for me to grasp, Jacki was the heartthrob of little Harry Ballsack. Fine by me.

Jacki asked a few follow-up questions, clarifying some of McAllister's prior testimony, and then shifted to the sole point we'd hoped to score with him.

"Professor, has the Missouri legislature done anything to—in your words—ameliorate some of the harshness of the Rule?"

McAllister gave Jacki a broad smile and nodded his head. "Excellent question, Ms. Brand. And the answer is yes. I would direct your attention—and the Court's attention—to Chapter 456.025(1) of the Missouri Revised Statutes."

"Please explain."

"That statute provides a simple way to steer clear of all of those hazards. As the express language of that statute provides, its sole purpose is to provide a way to avoid the Rule Against Perpetuities."

"Was that statute on the books when the property deed at issue was created?"

"Oh, yes, indeed. It has been the law of Missouri for decades."

"Could it have been used for this transaction?"

"Absolutely. If that bequest had been implemented as a trust under that statute, Ms. Brand, none of us would be here today."

"Thank you, Professor. I have no further questions."

Judge Ballsack leaned forward with a smile. "Thank you, Ms. Brand," he cooed.

His smile morphed into a frown as he turned toward Larry Blatz, who was already on his feet and heading toward the podium.

"Mr. Blatz?"

"Ready, willing, and able, Judge."

"Cut the infantile jokes, Counselor, and ask your questions."

Blatz saluted. "Yes, sir, Your Honor."

He turned to McAllister. "Good afternoon, sir."

McAllister nodded.

"This Rule Against Perpetuities—we've been hearing a lot about it, eh?"

"Apparently."

"Complex stuff, eh?"

McAllister frowned. "Compared to what, sir?"

Blatz chuckled. "Good point. Compared to other rules of property law."

"There are other rules that I would characterize as equally complex as the Rule Against Perpetuities."

"And other rules that are simpler, correct?"

"Yes."

"Do you devote any time in your property law class to teaching your students about the Rule Against Perpetuities?"

"Yes."

"How much time?"

"Generally, two lectures."

"So two classes, correct?"

"Yes."

"Why two?"

"To make sure my students fully grasp all of its elements, nuances, and risks."

"Lots of risks, eh?"

McAllister sighed. "Yes. That's one of the reasons I devote two lectures to the topic."

"Do you also tell your students about that Missouri statute regarding the use of trusts?"

"I do, indeed. I make sure my students understand all important aspects of that topic. I generally include a question about it on the final exam."

"So if a lawyer hadn't taken your class on property, he might be, shall we say, S-O-L."

McAllister frowned. "S-O-L?"

Blatz forced a chuckle as he scrambled for a G-rated answer. "You know, uh, So Out of Luck."

"Mr. Blatz, I am hardly the only law school professor that includes the Rule Against Perpetuities in his property law class."

"But you can speak authoritatively only about your class and your students, correct?"

McAllister considered the question and nodded. "I suppose you are correct."

Blatz grinned. "Yes, I believe I am. And now to my point, sir. We don't know who taught property law to the late Adam Fox, do we?"

McAllister smiled. "Apparently, one of us doesn't."

Blatz frowned. "Only one of us? Who?"

"Apparently you, sir."

"Do you know who taught him property law?"

"I do."

"Who would that be?"

"That would be me, Mr. Blatz. Adam was in my class his first year of law school."

For five long seconds, all eyes were on Blatz, who struck what could best be described as his deer-in-the-headlights pose.

"Well," he finally said, forcing a chuckle, "and how did he do in the class?"

"I checked his grade yesterday. I gave him a B."

The same grade McAllister gave Judge Ballsack. Even Blatz had enough sense to step back from that ledge.

He flipped through his legal pad, turned toward Norma Cross, who glared back him, arms crossed over her chest. He looked back down at his notes.

"Counsel?" the judge said.

Blatz looked up at the judge with a forced smile. "I think that's about all for me, Judge. Nothing further."

Chapter Thirty-eight

Sterling rested his case late that afternoon. By then, I'd concluded that we'd never be able to overcome the Rule Against Perpetuities. Jacki and I spent that evening planning our alternative strategy, which was part malpractice claim and part Larry Blatz hand grenade.

Marsha Knight was our first witness the following morning. Given Judge Ballsack's obvious crush on Jacki, I had her handle the direct examination. She and Marsha did it quite well, especially when they reached the most awkward part of the chronology of the divorce case.

"According to the court file," Jacki said, "Mr. Fox filed his appearance as your attorney in March of that year, correct?"

"That sounds right."

"How long had you known him by then?"

"Maybe a couple weeks."

"How did you select him?"

Marsha smiled. "Actually, he was selected for me."

"By whom?"

"Ms. Cross."

"Norma Cross?" Jacki turned toward Norma, who was seated next to Tom Sterling.

"Yes," Marsha said.

Jacki asked, "How did that happen?"

"I knew that I needed a good lawyer. Jerry—my husband, well, my ex-husband—had hired Irving Sliman as his lawyer. If he had Mr. Sliman, that meant I needed someone good. Really good. And tough. I'd seen those ads for Ms. Cross, and friends of mine told me she was the best in town. I made an appointment, we met, we talked about my situation, I came back the next day, she introduced me to Mr. Fox, told me he was a terrific lawyer and the perfect match for Irving Sliman." She shrugged. "What did I know? I'd never hired a lawyer before. I said okay. That's how he became my lawyer."

"The day that Norma Cross introduced you to Adam Fox— that was the first day you knew him, correct?"

"Yes."

"Mrs. Knight, at some point after that first day, after you established an attorney-client relationship with Mr. Fox, did your relationship with him change?"

Marsha blushed and looked down. "I'm embarrassed to say yes."

"Why embarrassed?"

"I was a mess back then. Jerry had dumped me for a younger woman. I was feeling pretty lousy. Vulnerable, I guess. Not that that's an excuse."

She took a deep breath and exhaled.

"Anyway," she continued, "one thing led to another, and before long we were—well, we were having an affair."

"A sexual affair?"

"Yes."

"How long did that last?"

"A little over a year."

"Did that relationship end before your divorce was final?"

"Yes."

"What happened?"

Marsha frowned. "I never really knew."

"What do you mean?"

"One day over lunch Adam told me we had to stop having, well, you know, we had to stop being intimate with each other."

"Did he say why?"

"No. He just said it wasn't wise for us to be in that sort of relationship while he was my lawyer. He said we should wait until the case was over, the divorce final."

"What was your reaction?"

Marsha took a deep breath, exhaled slowly, and shook her head. "Confusion. And pain. But mostly confusion."

"About what?"

"Adam just didn't seem himself. He seemed real nervous. Like he was under a lot of pressure or something."

"How close was this to the end of the case?"

"Real close. The divorce was final about a month later."

"Did you and Adam get back together after that?"

"No. I never heard from him again. I tried to call him. I left some messages on his phone. But he never called back."

"Did he break up with you before or after you signed the property settlement?"

"It was right before that."

"Did he advise you to sign it?"

"Yes. He told me it was a great deal."

"Did he tell you he tried to get the property put into a trust for you?"

She frowned. "He had mentioned something about a trust earlier, but he said this was a better way to go. He said I'd be able to avoid all the bureaucracy of a trust."

"So you signed it?"

"Yes."

"On his advice?"

"Yes."

"Did you rely on him and his advice?"

"Oh, yes. Definitely. I trusted him. And I remembered Ms. Cross telling me what a great lawyer he was."

"So you relied on her advice as well?"

"Yes. Definitely."

"In fact, I have here a copy of the final divorce decree." Jacki held up the order. "It's marked Exhibit F. May I please approach the witness, Your Honor?"

"Go right ahead, Ms. Brand. Go right ahead."

Jacki smiled at the judge and then walked over to the witness box to hand Marsha the copy of the final divorce order."

"Do you recognize Exhibit F, Ms. Knight?"

"I do."

"What is it?"

"It was the final order in my divorce case."

"Do you see the judge's signature and the date stamp?"

"I do."

"And beneath that are signature lines for your lawyer and for you ex-husband's lawyer."

"Yes."

"Who signed as the attorney for Mr. Knight?"

"Irving Sliman."

"And who signed that order as your attorney?"

"Norma Cross."

Jacki paused to let that answer sink in.

"One final topic, Ms. Knight. How did you find out that your husband knew about your affair with Adam Fox?"

"When Rachel Gold told me."

"When was that?"

"The day after she took Danielle's deposition."

"What did she tell you?"

Larry Blatz jumped up. "Objection. Hearsay."

Jacki turned to the judge. "I'll rephrase the question, Your Honor."

Ballsack smiled. "Very good, Ms. Brand. Proceed."

"Ms. Knight," Jacki said, "on the day after Danielle Knight's deposition, during your meeting with Rachel Gold, leaving aside whatever she may have told you, did she show you anything?"

"Yes."

"What did she show you?"

"The video of Danielle's deposition."

"Any particular portion?"

"Yes, the part where Danielle said that Jerry told her that I was having sex with Adam Fox."

"Thank you, Ms. Knight." Jacki turned toward the judge. "I have no further questions, Your Honor."

Ballsack smiled and nodded. "Well done, Ms. Brand. Mr. Sterling?"

Tom Sterling scratched his goatee as he mulled it over. After a long pause, he stood. "No questions for the witness, Judge."

Ballsack turned, with obvious displeasure, toward Larry Blatz. As Blatz started to rise, Norma Cross grabbed his arm and pulled him back down.

"Give me a moment, Judge," he said with a grin. "Got a check in here with the Big Kahuna."

After more than a minute of furious back and forth whispers, Blatz shrugged, nodded, and stood. "Well, I guess I have no questions, Judge."

The judge turned to Marsha. "You may step down, Mrs. Knight."

He turned to Jacki. "Another witness, Ms. Brand?"

"Yes, Your Honor."

Jacki turned to me.

I stood. "Defendant calls Professor Phoebe Hecht."

Chapter Thirty-nine

Phoebe Hecht was seated in the gallery. I smiled as I watched her come forward, step into the witness stand, and raise her right hand for the courtroom clerk to administer the oath. Although Phoebe Hecht was in her forties, she was still as adorable as a Gerber baby, with big blue eyes, a pug nose, pink cheeks, and curly fair hair cut in a bob. Cute but brilliant. And esteemed within her field of property law, as I made clear in my opening questions, during which, among other things, I introduced into evidence her curriculum vitae, which included a four-page listing of her published scholarly articles on a variety of topics in the field of property law.

My initial meeting with Phoebe, which Benny had arranged, made me realize that any battle to overcome the Rule Against Perpetuities might be a lost cause. Indeed, that meeting was the main reason I added the third-party claim against the Cross Law Firm. Phoebe's sole purpose today was to solidify our malpractice claim against Norma's firm, although much of that work had already been done by plaintiff's expert, Professor Hiram McAllister. And thus once I established her credentials as an expert, I had only a few questions.

"Do you cover the Rule Against Perpetuities in your property law class?"

"I do."

"Are all violations of that rule obvious?"

She smiled and shook her head. "Sadly, no. I spend most of one class going over some of the famous and convoluted hypotheticals, the ones where the fatal flaw can be hard to find, hidden within a grant that that seems simple and straightforward."

"Can you give the Court an example?"

"Certainly." She turned to the judge. "One of my favorites is the so-called fertile octogenarian."

"Can you explain?" I asked.

She smiled and nodded. "I'll warn you: it gets a little crazy."

"That's okay."

Judge Ballsack listened intently as she explained the hypothetical bequest to an eighty-five-year-old widow and, after her death, to the first of her children to reach twenty-five, and why it violated the Rule.

When she finished, I paused to let her explanation sink in—or, perhaps more accurately, to bob along the surface.

"So," I said, "application of the Rule can be tricky at times."

"Oh, yes. There can be obscure twists and turns."

"Is that always the case?"

"Fortunately, no. Most of the violations are easy to spot."

"Have you reviewed the property deed at issue?"

"I have."

"In your opinion, Professor, does it violate the Rule Against Perpetuities?"

"Absolutely."

"Is that violation obscure?"

"Not at all. I am surprised that Mrs. Knight's attorney missed it. Indeed, I don't understand how he could have missed it. I also don't understand why he didn't insist that property be handled via a trust."

"Why do you say that, Professor?"

"Quite simple. The Missouri legislature created that trust statute *solely* for the purpose of safeguarding against the Rule Against Perpetuities." She shook head. "Frankly, Ms. Gold, Mrs. Knight's lawyer failed in his duty to protect her."

Neither Sterling nor Blatz had any cross-examination.

After Professor Hecht left the witness stand, Jacki called Robert Dunlop, our commercial real estate appraiser. He was a familiar expert witness to Judge Ballsack and most of the other state court judges in St. Louis, having frequently testified in eminent domain cases and various real estate disputes. Jacki put him through the paces, established our $5.2 million number, and stood aside as Larry Blatz flailed away for fifteen minutes of useless cross-examination.

Once the judge excused Dunlop, I rested our case.

Sterling stepped forward and moved for judgment on his client's Rule Against Perpetuities claim against Marsha Knight. When he finished, I stepped back to the podium.

"Your Honor," I said, "if the Court should determine that the property grant to my client is void, then I move for judgment on my client's malpractice claim against the Cross Law Firm. The testimony of Professor McAllister and the testimony of Professor Hecht establish that my client is the innocent victim of gross malpractice on the part of her divorce attorney and his law firm."

Blatz practically sprinted to the podium after I stepped away. "Whoa!" He made his time-out signal. "These learned Counsel need to hold their horses. Their ejaculations over their motions are, frankly, premature, Judge. To quote the great Desi Arnaz, 'Lucy, you got some 'splainin' to do!'"

He leaned back with a triumphant grin and gave me a wink.

Ballsack glared down at him. "Mr. Blatz, unless you would like to be held in contempt—and by 'held' I mean in the holding cage where my bailiff will be happy to escort you—you'd better start over."

Blatz chuckled. "Just trying to add a little levity to the end of this long day, Judge. No harm intended. Quite simply, Counsel's two motions are premature. We will be putting on our case tomorrow, and I can assure Mr. Sterling and Ms. Gold that we will be rocking your world and knocking your socks off."

Judge Ballsack banged his gavel. "Enough! Mr. Blatz, you seem drawn to hackneyed expressions and metaphors. Well, I have one for you, sir, and it comes in the form of a warning: You are skating on thin ice. Very thin ice. Proceed with great caution or you may fall through and freeze to death."

The judge leaned back, shook his head, and announced, "We will resume tomorrow at ten a.m. sharp."

He banged his gavel twice. "Adjourned for the day."

He stood and disappeared through the door behind the bench.

I walked back to our counsel's table, where Marsha was helping Jacki gather and pack up our court papers.

"Well," Jacki said in a whisper, "I believe the pin has been pulled."

Chapter Forty

The first sign that Larry Blatz had shifted tactics was the absence of Daniel Crocker, the purported "legal malpractice expert" included on his "Will Call" witness list. He was not in the courtroom the following morning, and when asked, Blatz said Crocker was no longer needed. In other words, he wasn't going to seriously contest my malpractice claim against the Cross Law Firm.

The second sign of a shift in tactics was the absence of Shannon McCarthy, Adam Fox's sister, and the second of the two witnesses on Blatz's "Will Call" witness list. Then again, I told myself, he could be planning to put her on the witness stand later in the day.

The third—and most surprising—sign was the presence of Irving Sliman, seated in the back row of the gallery. He was wearing his courtroom attire: gray pinstriped suit, starched white shirt, dark bow tie, black horn-rimmed sunglasses.

The fourth and final sign, seated next to Sliman, was a man immediately recognizable with the scarlet yarmulke on his bald head, the neatly trimmed black goatee, the strong nose, and the tinted aviator glasses. Yes, Myron Dathan. One of the creepiest lawyers in St. Louis—cuddly as a tarantula, affable as a moray eel. Unfortunately, also one of the better lawyers in St. Louis—a brilliant litigator with an uncanny ability to detect his opponent's pressure points. Dathan and I had our own courtroom history: a nasty case involving the estate of Mendel Sofer, a Holocaust survivor—a case that ended poorly for Dathan and his clients. We hadn't spoken since then.

Irving Sliman was hunched over a yellow legal pad and scribbling notes as I passed by the two men on my way to counsel's table. I paused and nodded at Dathan.

"Good morning, Myron."

He stroked his goatee as he gazed at me with an expression that hovered somewhere between amusement and disdain—it was hard to tell which because his eyes were veiled behind those tinted lenses.

He nodded back. "Counsel."

Sliman looked up from his notes and smiled. "Good morning, Rachel."

When I reached counsel's table, where Jacki and Marsha were waiting, I looked back at Sliman and Dathan and then turned to Jacki.

"What is Dathan doing here? Is he a witness?"

"No," she said. "He's here as Slimeball's attorney."

"Huh?"

"That's what he told the courtroom clerk."

I looked over at the table where Larry Blatz and Norma Cross were seated. Larry looked at me, gestured toward the back of the courtroom, grinned, and gave me a wink.

I turned to the other counsel table—the one with Tom Sterling and Danielle Knight. Sterling had on a tan suit today, blue shirt, bolo tie, and cowboy boots. He gestured at two men in the gallery and gave me a shrug.

I turned to Jacki and Marsha. "Fasten your seatbelts, ladies."

"All rise!"

We stood as the door behind the judge's bench opened and little Harry Ballsack strode in, his black judicial robe flapping behind him. He took his seat, looked around the courtroom, banged his gavel, and announced, "Be seated."

He turned toward Larry Blatz. "Ready to proceed, Counsel?"

Larry jumped to his feet with a big grin. "To quote the late great Otis Redding, I'm sitting on the dock of the bay."

Ballsack frowned. "What in God's name is that supposed to mean?"

"All systems go, Your Honor. We are ready to launch. Shall I call my first witness?"

Ballsack sighed and shook his head in irritation. "Yes, Counsel. Let's get this moving."

"The Cross Law Firm calls to the stand one Irving Sliman."

Sliman and Dathan both stood and started toward the front of the courtroom. Sliman stepped to the witness box while Dathan walked over to the podium.

Judge Ballsack frowned. "Mr. Dathan?"

He smiled at the judge.

"Good morning, Your Honor," he said in that plummy baritone that some found soothing and I found smarmy. "It is always a true pleasure to be in this courtroom."

"Do you have some matter before the Court this morning?"

Dathan chuckled. "I do, indeed. I am here today to enter my appearance on behalf of my client, Irving Sliman."

Ballsack's frown deepened. "Mr. Dathan, your client is not a party in this lawsuit."

"You are most certainly correct, Your Honor. And I fully understand your bemusement. But as the Court is well aware, there are always delicate but vital issues of attorney-client privilege whenever a lawyer is called upon to testify concerning a matter in which he was once involved in his professional capacity. Such is the case here, where my client served as the attorney for the late Jerome Knight." Dathan paused and lowered his head. "*Alav ha-shalom.*"

"Huh?" Jacki whispered to me.

I shook my head in disgust.

Classic Dathan.

Among his many unpleasant qualities was how he exploited his religion—our religion—for strategic advantage. He used his encyclopedic knowledge of Jewish law to cancel hearings, halt depositions, terminate meetings, and otherwise refuse to cooperate; when challenged, he would curtly cite an obscure

Jewish holiday or custom that purportedly created the scheduling conflict. It was a technique designed to incapacitate Gentiles. And today's tactic was another one: baffling everyone in the court (except me) by pausing to solemnly recite a traditional Hebrew honorific for the dead, this one meaning, "May peace be upon him."

After that phony moment of silence, Dathan looked up and resumed. "Accordingly, Your Honor, it is imperative in such situations that there be independent counsel present during the proceeding to guard the sanctity of that attorney-client privilege. I am honored today to have been chosen to serve Mr. Sliman *and* our legal profession in that capacity."

Ballsack frowned, glanced over at Sliman, and then back at Dathan. "Very well, Mr. Dathan. Let's proceed."

The judge turned to the courtroom clerk. "You may swear in the witness."

As I watched the clerk administer the oath, I tried to figure out what Sliman's end game could be. Yes, he was angry with Danielle Knight for deserting his son as her attorney. And yes, he was angry with Norma Cross for, according to Jacki's account, humiliating his son in open court. But to seek revenge on the witness stand against either of those women brought with it great personal risk. The presence of Myron Dathan as his guardian angel—or perhaps guardian devil—added yet another layer of complexity to the situation.

The early phase of Blatz's examination was noteworthy primarily for how easily Sliman avoided admitting anything.

"At what point, Mr. Sliman, did you realize your proposed deed violated the Rule Against Perpetuities?"

"Violated?" Sliman frowned, his dark sunglasses hiding his eyes. "Has there been a ruling to that effect, Counsel? I thought the applicability of the Rule Against Perpetuities was the central *legal* issue in this proceeding. I am merely a fact witness, sir. I defer to our learned judge for such lofty determinations."

"Okay. Let's try it this way: Did you believe that your proposed deed violated the Rule Against Perpetuities?"

"I confess, Counsel, that I barely passed my Property Law course in law school. I am no more an expert on the Rule Against Perpetuities that I am an expert on Einstein's Theory of Relativity. As they say, it's all Greek to me."

"But you do know, sir, that Mr. Fox believed that your proposed deed violated the Rule Against Perpetuities, correct?"

"Objection," Dathan said. "Calls for speculation. Mr. Sliman is not a mind reader."

"Sustained."

Blatz looked down at his notes, hands clenching either side of the podium. Eventually, he looked up at the witness.

"Okay, sir, let's try it this way. During your negotiations with Mr. Fox over the divorce settlement, did he tell you that his issue with the deed could be resolved by Section 456.025 of the Missouri Revised Statutes?"

"Objection," Dathan said. "Hearsay and violation of the Dead Man's Act."

"Sustained."

Blatz looked down at his notes, and then opened a manila folder he had with him on the podium. He held up a paper-clipped set of documents. "Okay, okay. Let's give it a try this way. I present the witness with a document I have marked Cross Exhibit A."

He handed the document to Sliman, a copy to the courtroom clerk, and passed out copies to each of the attorneys.

Cross Exhibit A was the two-page transcription of that final telephone call between Sliman and Fox.

"Do you recognize Cross Exhibit A, sir?"

"I do."

"Can you tell me what it is?"

"Yes, I can."

Blatz waited, his expression gradually growing confused. "Well?"

"Well what, sir?"

"I asked you if you could tell me what Cross Exhibit A was?"

"You did. And I answered truthfully. I told you that I could."

Blatz exhaled slowly. "Okay. Then tell me. What is it?"

"It would appear to be a transcript, prepared by my secretary, of a telephone conversation between Mr. Fox and myself."

"Was that unusual?"

"Was what unusual?"

"Preparation of a transcript of a telephone conversation between you and opposing Counsel?"

"In general, yes. With respect to Mr. Fox, sadly, no."

"Why so, with Mr. Fox?"

"Because I learned early on that he was a mendacious and untrustworthy individual who was prone to misrepresentations and exaggerations, especially in court. In short, he was a standard member of the Cross Law Firm."

I glanced over at Norma Cross, who visibly stiffened.

Sliman continued. "His deceitful ways were all the more dangerous because of his innocent Boy Scout persona. Accordingly, I deemed it prudent to keep a record of our communications."

"And thus this exhibit."

Sliman nodded. "Correct."

"Do you see Mr. Fox's reference to Section 456.025 of the Missouri Revised Statutes in that transcript?"

"I do."

"Do you know what that Section is?"

"No."

"No?"

"No, and I don't even know if that is the correct citation."

"What do you mean?"

"This transcript was prepared by my secretary as she listened in on the speaker phone. She is not a trained court reporter or stenographer. And because very few of my opponents are dishonest and unreliable, she is seldom called upon to create these transcripts. While I rarely reviewed them for accuracy back then, the occasional time I did review one I would find a few mistakes. Thus I can't be sure if she correctly transcribed the Section number Mr. Fox cited."

Blatz backed away from the podium as he tried to collect his thoughts.

"Counsel?" the judge asked.

"Sorry." He stepped back to the podium. "Are you aware that the section of the Missouri statutes cited by Mr. Fox was enacted specifically to avoid the Rule Against Perpetuties?"

"No."

"Why do you think he cited it?"

Sliman shrugged. "I don't know. I don't remember. This was several years ago, Counsel."

"Look at the exhibit, sir. Do you see where he says that you should make that deed a trust? He says he checked. He says that Section 456.025 solves the issue. Do you see that?"

"I do."

"Does that refresh your recollection that Mr. Fox wanted you to make the deed a trust so that it would avoid the Rule Against Perpetuities?"

"No, it does not refresh my recollection."

"Look at what follows in the transcript."

"Okay."

"He says that the statute solves the issue. You tell him you hardly think so. You tell him your draft solves the issue because you checked the rules. He asks what rules. You answer, and I quote, 'Come on, Adam. We play by the rules.' Closed quote. And his answer—and I warn the Court there is a curse word in here—his answer is, quote 'You mean 4-1.8? Come on, Irving. This is bullshit.' Is that what he said?"

"So it appears."

"Can you tell the Court what you meant by Rule 4-1.8?"

"No."

"Why not?"

"Because I didn't say it. Mr. Fox did."

"What did he mean by it?"

"Objection," Dathan said. "Calls for speculation."

"Sustained."

After a pause, Blatz asked, "Did you understand what he was referring to?"

"I don't remember."

"Are you familiar with the Missouri Rules of Professional Responsibility?"

"Yes."

"Are you familiar with Rule 4-1.8?"

"Not off the top of my head."

"It covers conflicts of interest."

"If you say so."

"I don't say so, Mr. Sliman. The Rule says so."

Sliman smiled. "If you say so."

"Here. I am handing you a photocopy of the full text of Rule 4-1.8."

He handed a copy to Sliman, a copy to the courtroom clerk, and copies to each of the attorneys.

"Mr. Sliman, would you look at subsection (j) of Rule 4-1.8?"

"Okay."

"Please read it into the record, sir."

"Okay. 'A lawyer shall not have sexual relations with a client unless a consensual sexual relationship existed between them when the client-lawyer relationship commenced.'"

"At the time of the telephone call transcribed as Exhibit A, Mr. Sliman, you were aware that Mr. Fox was having sexual relations with his client, Mrs. Knight. Correct?"

Sliman appeared to ponder that question. "I had no personal knowledge of that fact."

"But you had been told of that fact by your own client, correct?"

"Objection," Dathan said. "Hearsay and the Dead Man's Act."

"Your Honor," Blatz said, "my question goes solely to Mr. Sliman's mental state, and not to the underlying truth of whatever his client told him."

Judge Ballsack frowned. "Overruled. You may answer, sir."

Sliman nodded. "Yes, my client told me that his wife was having sexual relations with Mr. Fox."

"And Mrs. Knight testified yesterday that her sexual relationship with Mr. Fox started after she had retained him and his law firm. That fact is undisputed."

"If you say so."

"Therefore, sir, did Mr. Fox's conduct with his client constitute a violation of Rule 4-1.8 of the Missouri Rules of Professional Conduct?"

"So it would appear."

"What are the consequences of a violation of subsection j of Rule 4-1.8?"

"I don't know." Sliman smiled. "I never violated it."

"A violator could be disbarred, correct?"

"Perhaps."

"And if not disbarred, then sanctioned severely, correct?"

"Perhaps."

"Mr. Sliman," Blatz said, pausing to stare at him, "did you threaten Mr. Fox with a disciplinary complaint over his sexual misconduct?"

"A disciplinary complaint?" Sliman appeared to mull over the question. "No, I did not."

"Did you tell him that if he didn't get his client to sign that deed you would file a disciplinary complaint against him with the Chief Disciplinary Counsel of the Missouri Bar?"

Sliman paused, repeating the question in his head. "No."

"Mr. Sliman, did you use that threat of disbarment to force Mr. Fox to betray his client and have her sign a deed that you knew violated the Rule Against Perpetuities and could someday be used to strip her of the entirety of her divorce settlement?"

"No."

"Hah! So you say. Your conduct, sir—was it anything other than classic extortion?"

"Objection, Your Honor." Dathan turned to Blatz and shook his head in disapproval. "I am shocked. Shocked, sir. If any conduct is worthy of a disciplinary action, it is Counsel's intemperate behavior, including these wild and defamatory accusations against my client. I would urge the Court to remind Counsel that this courtroom is no place for the airing of delusional calumny."

Blatz raised his hand. "No need, Your Honor. I've more than made my point. I'm done with this witness. Over and out."

As Blatz started to walk away, Dathan stepped up to the podium. "I have a few questions, Your Honor."

Blatz turned back. "What? This is nuts. Mr. Dathan does not represent a party in this case."

"Judge," Dathan said, "my client has been an esteemed member of the bar for nearly half a century. Having retired after an illustrious career, he has been forced to sit in that witness box as Mr. Blatz has hurled one baseless invective after another. I beg the Court's indulgence so that I may ask Mr. Sliman a few clarifying questions before he steps down."

"Fine," Ballsack snapped. "Make it quick."

"Thank you, Your Honor." Dathan turned to Sliman. "If I understand your testimony, sir, at some point during your representation of Mr. Knight in the divorce proceedings your client told you that Mrs. Marsha Knight was having sexual relations with her attorney, correct?"

"Yes."

"Did you file a complaint with the Chief Disciplinary Counsel of the Missouri Bar regarding the misconduct of Mr. Fox?"

"I did not."

"Why not, sir?"

"He was my adversary. Perhaps I am old school, Mr. Dathan, but it seemed somewhat uncouth to file a bar complaint against your adversary in the midst of that proceeding."

"Did you ever file a complaint against Mr. Fox?"

"No."

"Did you do anything regarding his misconduct?"

"Yes."

"What did you do?"

"I told his boss."

Dathan turned to Norma Cross. "You mean Ms. Cross?"

"Yes."

"When did you tell her?"

"After the divorce was final. After my dealings with Mr. Fox had concluded. I believe it was a few months later."

"Where did you tell her?"

"At the St. Louis Club. I had my secretary set up a meeting for late in the afternoon."

"What made you decide to tell Ms. Cross instead of filing a complaint?"

"I thought long and hard about that issue, Mr. Dathan. Ms. Cross was his boss, and presumably she had been actively involved in supervising him in the Knight divorce. After all, her name appears above his in the signature block in all court filings in that matter. Thus I believed that the responsible thing to do was to inform Ms. Cross and let her decide how to handle Mr. Fox's ethical transgression."

"What was Ms. Cross' reaction when you informed her of Mr. Fox's misconduct?"

"My goodness. She was quite upset. She did not say much at the meeting, but I could sense that she felt betrayed—betrayed on a deeper level than I had imagined."

"How so?"

"Her anger seemed personal. Very personal and very emotional. She told me she would take care of it and then stormed out of our meeting."

"Did you hear back from her?"

"No."

"Did she take care of it?"

"You'll have to ask her. All I do know is that a few weeks after that meeting with Ms. Cross, Mr. Fox was dead."

Dathan turned to the judge. "Your Honor, I have nothing further for the witness."

"But I do!"

We turned toward Blatz's table, where he was still seated. The speaker, standing and red-faced, was Norma Cross.

She said, "I certainly have something further for this witness."

The judge stared at her. "What do you mean?"

Norma strode to the podium. "I have some questions of my own for Mr. Sliman."

The judge frowned. "You are the client, Ms. Cross."

"I am also an attorney." She was furious. "And I have questions for this witness."

"But you have an attorney in this matter."

"He is not my attorney. I did not choose him. The insurance company did."

Blatz stood, forcing a smile. "Well, Judge—"

"Sit down!" Cross ordered.

Blatz obeyed, eyes wide.

Chapter Forty-one

Standing at the podium, Norma Cross glared at Irving Sliman in the witness box. Behind his dark sunglasses, Sliman appeared to gaze back at her calmly.

She said, "Adam Fox told you he wanted the property transfer to Mrs. Knight to be done by a trust, correct?"

"So it would appear from this transcript."

"He said his concern was easy to resolve, correct?"

Sliman looked down at the transcript. "If that portion of the transcript is accurate, then the answer is yes. I don't personally recall that, but it's been many years since that conversation."

"And this concern of Mr. Fox was that your deed violated the Rule Against Perpetuities, correct?"

Sliman read the two-page transcript. "No, he didn't say that. He didn't mention the Rule Against Perpetuities."

"But he cited the statute that was designed to solve that problem, right? The one that enables you to avoid the Rule Against Perpetuities by making the transfer via a trust, correct?"

Sliman shrugged. "He apparently cited a Missouri statute, Counsel. I don't know what it says, and, according to this transcript, he didn't explain it to me."

"Look at the transcript, Mr. Sliman. He cited that statute and then he said, and I quote, 'It solves the issue,' close quote. Correct?"

"According to this transcript."

"And the issue was the Rule Against Perpetuities, correct?"

Sliman studied the transcript. "Again, Ms. Cross, I don't see that rule mentioned."

"Quit playing word games."

Sliman stared back at Cross. "I think you may be the one playing word games, Counsel. I'm sticking with what is in this transcript. Many years have passed since then. I confess that my memory isn't what it once was. But fortunately we have this contemporary record of my conversation with Mr. Fox. My secretary may not have gotten down every word, but I'm fairly sure that she got the gist."

"We all got the gist, Mr. Sliman. And the gist is that you were blackmailing Mr. Fox, correct? Make Marsha Knight sign this defective deed, you were saying, or I will file a disciplinary complaint against you and destroy your career."

"Blackmail, Ms. Cross?" Sliman asked, his tone calm. "My goodness, Counsel. Those are strong words."

"Do you prefer extortion, sir? Or shall we call it a good old-fashioned shakedown?"

"Objection." Dathan stepped to the podium, a stern look on his face. "Good heavens, Your Honor. Ms. Cross has traversed all boundaries of decency here. This slander is nothing short of intentional infliction of emotional distress in the guise of cross-examination. I expressly reserve the right to restore Mr. Sliman's reputation before he is dismissed as a witness."

"Objection sustained. Rein it in, Ms. Cross. If you have a genuine question to ask, ask it. Otherwise, sit down."

Ignoring the judge, Cross continued to stare at Sliman. He gazed back her, unruffled.

"Counsel?" the judge asked. "Either ask a question or sit down."

"And when it was all over," Cross said, still staring at Sliman, "and when Mrs. Knight had signed the deed and the divorce decree had been entered and sufficient time had passed to make that decree final and beyond the deadline for an appeal—in short, when nothing could be done to undo what you had accomplished—you contacted me, correct?"

"You lost me somewhere in there, Ms. Cross."

She turned to the court reporter. "Read him my question."

The court reporter did so.

Sliman shrugged. "I still can't follow that timeline. All I do recall is that you and I did meet after the case was over."

"At your request, correct?"

"I believe so."

"We have the e-mail from your secretary to me requesting that meeting, Mr. Sliman."

"Okay."

"That e-mail is roughly three months after the judge entered the divorce decree."

"Okay."

"In other words, beyond the time for any appeal."

"If you say so."

"We met at the St. Louis Club, correct?"

"I believe we did."

"And during that meeting you never once mentioned the Rule Against Perpetuities, correct?"

"Correct."

"But you did tell me that Mr. Fox was having sex with his client during the course of the divorce proceedings, correct?"

"Correct."

"You told me that because you believed it was unethical, correct?"

"I was concerned that it might be."

Cross gave him an incredulous look. "Might be? Really?"

"Yes, I was concerned that it might be an ethical violation."

"But you never filed a complaint against him, correct?"

"Correct."

She shook her head in anger. "And what did you expect me to do?"

Sliman smiled. "I didn't expect you to do anything one way or the other. I felt it was my duty to provide you with notice of the misconduct of your employee. Period. What you did with that information was entirely up to you." He tilted his head slightly and smiled. "By the way, Ms. Cross, what exactly did you do with that information?"

"You are the witness, Mr. Sliman. I ask the questions, not you."

"Would you prefer not to answer my question, Ms. Cross? And if so, why?"

"That's all." She turned to the judge. "I'm done with this witness."

She spun on her heels and stomped back to her seat.

All eyes turned to Judge Ballsack, who sat motionless, a baffled look on his face. He looked down at this notes, then up toward the clock on the back wall, and then he raised his gavel. "Court will be in lunch recess. We will resume at one-thirty."

Bang!

"All rise!" cried the bailiff.

Chapter Forty-two

Marsha Knight, Jacki, and I exited the courtroom on our way to lunch.

"Rachel, dear."

I turned.

Seated on a bench in the hallway on the far side of the courtroom doors were Irving Sliman and Myron Dathan. Sliman was paging through some notes on a legal pad, head down, sunglasses pushed back on his bald head.

Dathan stood and gestured, giving me one of his smarmy smiles. "A moment of your time?"

I looked up at Jacki, who raised her eyebrows.

"Rachel, dear," she mimicked.

"Let's go see what he wants." I turned to Marsha. "Wait here. We'll be right back."

As Jacki and I approached, Dathan stepped toward one of the attorney conference rooms. He held the door open as we entered, closed the door behind him, and turned to us.

"What is it, Myron?" I said.

"I believe Mr. Blatz will rest his case after we return to court, assuming—" and here he chuckled "—that his client doesn't fire him during the lunch recess."

"He has one more witness on his list," I said. "Shannon McCarthy, Adam's sister."

"He will not be calling her, Rachel."

"How do you know?"

"Call it a wild guess." Another chuckle. "Let us assume that I am correct and that Blatz does indeed rest his case after lunch."

"Okay."

"I would like you to call Norma Cross to the witness stand," Dathan said.

I frowned. "Why?"

"If you didn't already plan to call her, I am certain that you can dream up a valid reason to ask a few questions. After all, she is the head of her law firm—indeed, its sole proprietor, and you have sued that firm for malpractice."

"And proven my claim, too. Again, Myron…why?"

He smiled. "I have a few questions for the lady, and since my client is not an actual party to this lawsuit, I need a pretext to examine her."

"So I'm the pretext?"

"In a way, yes. But you'll be quite pleased with the result."

"And again, Myron, why?"

"Why what?"

"Why do you want Norma on the stand? What do you want to ask her?"

"I can't answer that, Rachel. Attorney-client privilege. But you will be pleased with the results. I promise that my questions will in no way harm your claim, and in all likelihood her answers will strengthen your client's position." He raised his right hand. "I swear to you on *Hashem* that this will be so."

Hashem is the term Orthodox Jews use for God.

"What makes you think Judge Ballsack will let you ask her any questions?"

He smiled. "Irving feels confident regarding that issue." He chuckled. "Quite confident."

I shrugged. "I suppose I have a few questions for her."

"Excellent."

Jacki stepped forward. "That promise of yours, Myron? The one we're relying on?"

Dathan looked up at Jacki, who towered over him. "Yes, Miss Brand?"

"The one you pledged on that Hash thing."

"*Hashem.*"

"You better not break that promise."

Dathan scratched his goatee. "I don't plan to."

"Because if you do break it, Myron, you will regret it."

Dathan raised his eyebrows. "Is that so?"

"Oh, yes." Jacki leaned forward. "I will personally make you regret it."

"And exactly how would you propose to do that?"

"For starters, I will shove your head so far up your ass that when you fart your lips will quiver."

Dathan forced a smile. "That would be quite an anatomical accomplishment, Miss Brand. But until then, young lady, to quote my Bobba Eva, *Vaksn zolstu vi a tsibele mitn kop in dr'erd.*"

And he turned, opened the door, and left.

I looked up at Jacki. "Lips will quiver, eh? Benny would be proud."

"What an arrogant dick. And what was that gibberish he said at the end?"

"An old Yiddish curse. My grandmother used to say it."

"What's it mean?"

"May you grow like an onion with your head in the ground."

Jacki repeated it to herself silently. She smiled. "Not bad."

"Let's go get Marsha," I said. "We can fill her in over lunch."

Chapter Forty-three

Dathan was right. Larry Blatz rested his case after the lunch recess.

Judge Ballsack turned first to Tom Sterling. "Anything further, Counsel?"

Sterling stepped to the podium. "Nothing further, Your Honor. Plaintiff rests."

Ballsack turned to me. "Ms. Gold?"

"We have one rebuttal witness, Your Honor." I stepped to the podium. "Defendant calls to the stand Norma Cross."

Norma turned to Blatz, puzzled. He shrugged. She stood, adjusted her skirt, walked around counsel's table, and gave me an icy stare before she stepped toward the witness stand.

As the courtroom clerk began administering the oath, I turned again toward the courtroom gallery, trying to make sense of the four new faces there. Three I recognized, one I didn't. The latter was a middle-aged woman in a cream-colored blouse and navy pantsuit seated on the right side of the center aisle in the third row from the front. She'd been reading something on her iPhone when I walked past her toward the front of the courtroom.

Of the three that I did recognize, they were, in increasing order of surprise, Duncan O'Malley, Shannon McCarthy, and Detective Mario "Mouse" Aloni.

"...you do solemnly swear..."

Duncan O'Malley, seated in the second row, was the longtime courthouse reporter for the *St. Louis Post-Dispatch*. Perhaps it had been a slow news day in the courts—or perhaps someone had told him that the legendary Irving Sliman had been on the witness stand that morning and O'Malley was hoping to catch some Sliman testimony this afternoon.

"…that the testimony you are about to give in this matter…"

Shannon McCarthy, Adam Fox's sister, was seated in the fifth row along the right side. Perhaps Blatz had failed to let her know in advance that he wasn't going to call her as a witness, and, after finding out, she'd decided to stick around as a spectator.

"…shall be the truth, the whole truth…"

Detective Aloni was seated on the far left side of the back row. All I could think was maybe a prosecutor had called him to court on an unrelated matter that would be heard before our trial resumed—perhaps an emergency request for a search warrant. Such matters typically were heard right after lunch recess. Perhaps the prosecutor was running late.

"…and nothing but the truth."

"I do," Norma said.

"You may be seated," Judge Ballsack told her.

I turned toward the witness. "Good afternoon, Ms. Cross."

She nodded curtly.

I said, "I want to make sure that the Court and I correctly understand your position today. Should the Court determine that the property grant at issue here is invalid because of the Rule Against Perpetuities—a determination that would trigger my client's malpractice claim against your law firm—and should the Court then determine that your firm's representation of my client constitutes malpractice, is it your position that Adam Fox himself was a victim of extortion by Mr. Sliman?"

"Absolutely."

"In other words, you contend that Mr. Sliman was the proximate cause of any malpractice, correct?"

"Absolutely."

"Stated simply, you blame Mr. Sliman, and not Mr. Fox, for my client's predicament."

"Absolutely."

"And thus," I said, "if your firm is held liable for the damages suffered by my client, you contend that your firm would have a claim against Mr. Sliman."

"Absolutely."

I glanced down at my notes. I'd covered all my topics. I looked up at Norma, who was glaring at me, and back down at my legal pad. *Might as well have a little fun*, I said to myself.

I looked up at Norma. "Finally, Ms. Cross, you've heard the expert witness testimony on the Rule Against Perpetuities, correct?"

"Yes."

"In light of that testimony, can we all agree that you and your law firm did a terrible job representing my client?"

"Absolutely not!"

"I see. So is it your testimony that your law firm is perfectly fine with having its clients sign property settlements that are fatally defective?"

"Absolutely not!"

"Okay. Help me understand. Is it your testimony that clients of the Cross Law Firm should not expect their attorneys to have even the most basic knowledge of property law?"

"Absolutely not!"

I smiled. "Thank you, Ms. Cross."

I turned to the judge. "Nothing further."

As I returned to my seat, Ballsack looked over at Larry Blatz. "Any follow-up, Counsel?"

"Nope."

Ballsack turned to Tom Sterling. "Questions for the witness?"

"None, Your Honor."

By then, Myron Dathan was standing at the podium. "I do have a few questions of my own, Your Honor."

Blatz jumped to his feet. "Whoa, Nellie! I most certainly object. Mr. Dathan is present today solely as Mr. Sliman's lawyer.

I remind Counsel and the Court that Mr. Sliman is not a party to this case. He is merely a fact witness, and he has already testified."

"Your Honor," Dathan said, "this woman has impugned my client's integrity and besmirched his reputation. That bell, once rung, cannot be unrung. If I may borrow from the Bard, she who steals my client's purse steals trash; but she who filches from my client his good name robs him of that which does not enrich her and makes my client poor indeed. Accordingly, I request the Court's indulgence here."

Leave it to Dathan, I told myself, *to find inspiration in a line from Iago.*

The judge nodded, lips pursed, as if he were actually contemplating the issue instead of pretending to do so, presumably having already discussed this topic with Irving Sliman during the lunch recess.

"You may proceed, Mr. Dathan," Ballsack said.

"Thank you, Your Honor." Dathan turned to Norma Cross. "So, Ms. Cross, my client is the bad guy, eh?"

Norma crossed her arms over her chest. "Yes."

"And you, yourself, Ms. Cross? You claim innocence?"

"I most certainly do. I had no idea that your client was blackmailing my associate."

Dathan smiled. "Ah, yes, and you also had no idea that your associate was sleeping with someone other than yourself, correct?"

Norma frowned as she parsed that sentence. She turned to the court reporter. "Could you read back the last question?"

The court reporter lifted the ribbon of paper, found her place, and cleared her throat. "Ah, yes," she read in her court reporter monotone, "and you also had no idea that your associate was sleeping with someone other than yourself, correct?"

Norma turned back toward Dathan. "I had no idea," she said slowly and deliberately, "that my associate was sleeping with Mrs. Knight."

Dathan chuckled. "A good answer, Ms. Cross, but not to the question I asked. Madame Court Reporter, could you read my question to the witness one more time? And I would ask the Court to instruct the witness to answer my question."

"Yes," Judge Ballsack said, "listen to the question, Ms. Cross."

And once again the court reporter read the question: "Ah, yes, and you also had no idea that your associate was sleeping with someone other than yourself, correct?"

"I can't answer that question," Norma said.

"Pray tell, why not?"

"It assumes a fact not in evidence."

"And what fact is that?"

"That I was sleeping with Mr. Fox."

Dathan chuckled. "Good point, Ms. Cross. We should not assume a fact not yet in evidence. So let us put that fact into evidence. Were you having sexual relations with Mr. Fox during the time he was representing Mrs. Knight?"

A pause. "I don't recall the period during which Mr. Fox was representing Mrs. Knight."

"Let's make this easy. Did you ever have sex with Mr. Fox?"

"That's none of your business."

"Objection!" Blatz shouted. "This attempted invasion of my client's privacy is entirely unwarranted."

Judge Ballsack frowned. "Mr. Dathan," he said, shaking his head, "you appear to be going far afield here. How are you planning to connect this line of inquiry to any issue in the case?"

"I would ask the Court's indulgence. I have only a few more questions for this witness. But before I proceed, I would respectfully request that the Court provide Ms. Cross with a summary of her Miranda rights."

Ballsack lurched back in his chair, eyes wide. "What?"

"Please, Your Honor." And here he paused, looked back toward Detective Aloni, and then turned back to the judge. "I believe we are about to move into a territory where such a recital is appropriate."

Ballsack frowned. "Just a minute."

He shuffled through some papers on his desk.

Jacki leaned in close to me and whispered, "That pin has most definitely been pulled."

I nodded.

"Okay." Ballsack was squinting at an index card in his hand. "Ms. Cross, the Court advises you that you have the right to remain silent. Anything you do say can and may be used against you in a court of law. You have the right to have an attorney present before and during—well, you already have one present. Never mind that. And if you cannot afford the services of an attorney— well, that one doesn't apply either. There you go, Mr. Dathan. I have honored your bizarre request. Proceed, and hurry it up."

Dathan nodded and turned back to Norma. "Ms. Cross, you were here earlier when my client, Mr. Sliman, testified, correct?"

Norma looked confused. She glanced over at Blatz and then back at Dathan.

"Ms. Cross?" Dathan said.

She frowned. "What?"

"I'll repeat the question. You were here earlier when my client testified, correct?"

She paused, seemingly repeating the question in her head. "Yes, I was."

"You heard him testify about the meeting he had with you at the St. Louis Club approximately three months after the conclusion of the Knight divorce case, correct?"

"Yes."

"Did you find any of his testimony about that meeting inaccurate?"

She mulled that over. "Not that I recall."

"He said you were visibly angry and upset when he told you about your associate's sexual relations with Mrs. Knight, correct?"

"Absolutely. I was, and justifiable so."

"Why is that?"

"I had learned that Mr. Fox had engaged in conduct that was in violation of the Code of Professional Responsibility."

"And you were also upset to learn that your associate was cheating on you with another woman, correct?"

She leaned back in her chair and shook her head. "Certainly not."

"That didn't bother you? That he was cheating on you?"

"You are disgusting, Dathan. I'm not answering that question."

Dathan chuckled. "I believe you just did, Ms. Cross. But let's move ahead to the morning of his death. Just you and him on that hike in Castlewood State Park, correct?"

"Yes. It was one of the team-building exercises. Nothing unusual. I do several of those a year, each involving some form of vigorous and challenging activity."

"But normally those exercises involve several members of your firm, correct?"

"Some do, some don't."

"But this time—just the two of you, correct?"

"So what?"

"You brought donuts and coffee that morning, correct?"

"I don't recall."

"You even told Mr. Fox in advance that you were bringing donuts and Starbucks coffee, correct?"

"I don't recall."

"Did you know that Mr. Fox sent his sister a text the night before that hike in which he told his sister that you told him that you were bringing donuts and Starbucks coffee?"

"How would I know what he texted his sister?"

"If you look into the courtroom gallery, Ms. Cross, you will see Shannon McCarthy. As you know, she is Mr. Fox's sister. She has brought her smartphone to court today. At my request. She will testify, if necessary, that her brother sent her that text regarding the donuts and the Starbucks coffee. Does that refresh your recollection?"

Norma Cross was showing signs of unease. "No, it does not refresh my recollection. But if that's what he told her I said, then I suppose that's what I said."

"Did you bring those donuts?"

"I think so."

"And the Starbucks coffee?"

"Probably."

"Probably?"

"Yes," she said, a bit more defiantly. "Probably."

"And what did you put in his coffee?"

"What did I put in his coffee? As I recall, he liked his coffee black."

"That wasn't my question, Ms. Cross. Listen carefully. What did you put in his coffee?"

"I just told you. He liked his coffee black."

"So you did not put any cream in his cup?"

She snorted. "Of course not."

"And you did not put any sugar in there?"

She gave him an exasperated look. "Of course not."

"And no artificial sweetener?"

"Of course not."

"What about gamma-hydroxybutyric acid?"

Cross frowned. "What about what?"

"It's a drug, Ms. Cross. Known more commonly by its initials: GHB."

Cross stared at him.

Finally, Dathan said, "Well, Ms. Cross. Did you? Did you add some GHB to his coffee?"

Cross turned her gaze toward the empty jury box. "No."

Dathan said, "You understand you are under oath, Ms. Cross. Did you add some GHB to his coffee?"

Still staring at the jury box, she said, "No."

"And when you and Mr. Fox reached the top of those bluffs, and after the drug had taken effect and made him drowsy and off-balance, did you shove him off that cliff to his death?"

"No."

"So you deny you killed him?"

She turned back to Dathan. "Yes, I deny it."

"So be it." Dathan shook his sadly. "We have your answers, and they are all under oath. Nothing further, Your Honor."

After a clearly shaken Norma Cross returned to counsel's table, Dathan announced, "We have one final witness, Your Honor, a witness whose testimony is now essential to this case and to the cause of justice. We call to the stand Dr. Muriel Gilberg."

The woman in the navy pantsuit stood and stepped forward. She was carrying a folder. As she passed by, I could make out three words on the folder label: FOX AUTOPSY REPORT.

"Please state your name, Doctor."

"Murial Gilberg."

"What is your occupation?

"I am a professor of clinical pathology at the School of Medicine at the University of Missouri."

Section 6

*Man begins in dust and ends in dust—
meanwhile, it's good to drink some vodka.*

—Yiddish proverb

Chapter Forty-four

It was a Wednesday night about a month after the two trials ended. The four of us were seated around my kitchen table—Benny, my mother, Abe Rosen, and me.

Abe was there at Benny's special request.

"What am I?" Benny had demanded last week. "Chopped liver? You're dating a nice Jewish boy—better yet, according to your mother, a Jewish doctor—and I still haven't had a chance to vet him? It's time I meet this dude."

So I set up a potluck dinner for us. I made the salad and the sides. My mother baked her chocolate babka. Abe brought the drinks—a bottle of Malbec, a bottle of Chardonnay, and a six-pack of beer. Benny insisted on bringing the entrée, which consisted of two large bags of barbecue takeout from Sugarfire: ribs (four slabs), pulled pork, smoked brisket, and a half-dozen spiced pork sausages that Benny claimed were so celestial that they would have caused Rabbi Akiva to create a special exemption in the laws of kashrut.

Benny's vetting seemed to be going well. Sam had been awake when the three of them arrived. While I was upstairs putting Sam to bed, my mother went into the kitchen on some pretext, leaving Benny and Abe alone. When I came back downstairs, Benny was laughing over something Abe had said.

And on our way into the kitchen, Benny had pulled me aside. "That boy's a keeper."

Over dinner I'd filled them in on the latest, and increasingly curious, developments in Marsha Knight's Rule Against Perpetuities battle. The last witness in the case had been Dathan's pathologist, Dr. Muriel Gilberg. Her presence confirmed what I had suspected, namely, that the other person who'd obtained a copy of the Adam Fox autopsy report—the person Detective Aloni declined to identify to me—was Irving Sliman. Dr. Gilberg's opinion confirmed what my pal Izzy Feigelman had already concluded: that Adam Fox had imbibed an abnormally large quantity of GBH the morning he died.

The trial ended after Dr. Gilberg's testimony. Judge Ballsack took a one-hour recess, and when he returned he issued his rulings from the bench. Specifically, he (1) invalidated the property bequest to Marsha Knight, thus restoring ownership of that apartment complex to Jerry Knight's widow, Danielle, (2) entered judgment in Marsha Knight's favor on her malpractice claim against the Cross Law Firm, and (3) awarded her $5.2 million in damages.

Although those three rulings did find their way into Duncan O'Malley's front page article in the next morning's *St. Louis Post-Dispatch*, they were buried in a paragraph after the jump on page sixteen. As with the opening paragraphs of the story, the headline focused on a different aspect of the lawsuit's conclusion:

BIZARRE ENDING TO POST-DIVORCE LAWSUIT:
Prominent Divorce Lawyer Implicated
in Death of Alleged Boyfriend; Taken
Into Custody for Questioning

Norma had been questioned for several hours, but she'd been released later that evening without any charge.

Yet.

According to Detective Aloni, quoted in the follow-up story, "the investigation is ongoing." Norma Cross has since retained one of our town's top criminal defense lawyers, who told Channel 5 News that his client "was as innocent as the freshly fallen snow." I'm told he said that with a straight face.

Nevertheless, I've been around long enough to know the challenges a prosecutor will face if and when Norma gets indicted. Real life is not an episode of *Law & Order*. Proving homicide with just circumstantial evidence would be a challenge, especially if the investigators are unable to link Norma to the purchase of the GBH detected in the post-mortem blood of Adam Fox. Nevertheless, there are rumors of ongoing plea bargaining negotiations.

Meanwhile, Myron Dathan, presumably hoping to fend off any disciplinary charges against his client over the extortion allegations and to deter any lawsuit by the Cross Law Firm, launched his own public relations offensive, describing Irving Sliman as "a true white knight" who, at great personal risk, "sought to shine the bright light of justice on the sordid circumstances surrounding the tragic death of an innocent young man."

As for me, my responses to Duncan O'Malley's requests for quotes have been consistent: in all three of his articles, the following sentence appears: "Ms. Knight's trial attorney, Rachel Gold, declined to comment."

"How is Marsha doing?" Abe asked.

"She's doing okay," I said. "Ironically, an award of money is a better result for her than having to deal with all the managerial issues surrounding that property."

"But will she get paid?" my mother asked.

"The judgment is against the Cross Law Firm," I said. "They have three million in malpractice insurance. The carrier has agreed to pay the full amount of the policy. They'd rather be done with the case now instead of incurring the additional expense and risk of an appeal. We should have that check next week."

"What about the rest?" my mother said. "I thought the judge awarded more than five million dollars?"

"He did. The law firm is a sole proprietorship. That means Norma is personally on the hook for the rest."

"But will she pay it?" my mother asked.

"Good question." I smiled. "We've turned the answer to that question over to Sonny Sardino."

Benny laughed. "Fucking aye! I love it."

"Who is Sonny Sardino?" Abe asked.

"Norma Cross' worst nightmare," Benny said. "Sardino is the debt collector from hell. He's known around town as Sonny the Shark."

Samuel "Sonny" Sardino, Jr., now in his fifties, had started off as a smalltime collection lawyer for one of his uncles, a used car dealer in North County. Brilliant, savvy, and relentless, his reputation grew, as did the quantity and quality of his clients. He now represents national banks, art dealers, high-end jewelers, plaintiff's personal injury lawyers, and others chasing wealthy deadbeats.

"Sonny seemed particularly eager to take on this case," I said.

"Really?" my mother asked.

I smiled. "Guess who represented his former wife in their divorce case?"

"Beautiful," Benny said. "At least there's some justice in this world. When he gets done with Norma, she'll wish she'd been indicted."

We finished dinner. Abe and Benny put the dishes in the dishwasher while I boiled water for tea. When we returned to the table, my mother had given each of us a large slice of chocolate babka.

"Mom," I said, pointing at my dessert plate, "this is humongous. No one can eat this much."

"No one?" My mother turned to Benny. "Nu?"

"Looks just about the right size to me."

"That's because you could eat the entire cake," I said.

"And your point is?"

I poured each of us a cup of tea and took a seat.

"By the way," I said, "guess who wants to see Cyndi Mulligan and her daughter, Carson?"

"Let me think," Benny said. He took a forkful of the babka and washed it down with some tea. "Rush Limbaugh?"

"I'm serious, Benny."

"I give up. Who, pray tell, wants to see Cyndi and little Carson?"

"The biological father."

"The Grim Reaper, eh?" Benny said.

"That horrible son who sued her?" My mother shook her head in disgust. "*Trinkn zoln im piavkes.*"

Benny chuckled. "That sounds like a doozy, Sarah."

Abe smiled. "It is a good one."

Benny turned to Abe. "You speak Yiddish?"

"My grandmother did. She lived with us."

"So tell us what the sweet and gentle Sarah Gold has wished upon Bert Grimsley."

"That leeches should suck him dry."

"Absolutely," my mother said. "The sooner the better. Okay, who needs more babka?"

Benny raised hand. "Me."

"What did your client say?" Abe asked. "Is she going to let him see his daughter?"

"Not yet. Grimsley called her last week to apologize for everything. He asked permission to come visit."

"And?" Benny said.

"She told him no. Told him it was too soon."

"What do you think?" Abe said. "Should she?"

I leaned back in my chair and frowned. "I don't know. He's a total creep. Total. But he is Carson's father. And thanks to his own father, he'll never be able to have a kid of his own."

Benny took a sip of tea and shook his head. "Old Bert was one first-class prick. That bloodline trust scheme was brutal. Like throwing down a challenge to his son, who picked it up and walked right into a buzz saw. Even worse, the old bastard stole his own son's sperm in the process. All of it."

"I feel bad for Cyndi," I said. "Her own husband used her to get revenge on his son."

"Nothing's black and white," Abe said. "Your client wanted to have her husband's baby. Once he died, the closest she was ever going to get to that baby was through his son's sperm. She didn't know it back then, of course, but look how it turned out. She has a healthy daughter in the same bloodline as her husband. At least twenty-five percent of that little girl's genes are from her husband."

"And," Benny added, "that little girl is going to be set for life."

I shrugged. "I suppose."

I took a sip of tea.

I shook my head.

"What?" Benny asked.

"D.F.W.B."

He nodded. "Fucking zombies."

To which my mother added, "Some more babka, Benny?"

"How can I say no to you, Sarah?"

I looked across the table at Abe, gestured toward Benny, and rolled my eyes.

Abe smiled, reached across the table, and took my hand in his. I gave it a squeeze.

To receive a free catalog of Poisoned Pen Press titles, please provide your name, address, and e-mail address in one of the following ways:

Phone: 1-800-421-3976
Facsimile: 1-480-949-1707
Email: info@poisonedpenpress.com
Website: www.poisonedpenpress.com

Poisoned Pen Press
6962 E. First Ave. Ste 103
Scottsdale, AZ 85251